ANDERSON'S ROUNDUP

BY

TERRY MAY

ROCK HILL PUBLISHING

Published by: Rock Hill Publishing

ISBN: 978-0-9831817-5-0

For Becky and Shauna

CHAPTER 1

Hub Anderson climbed down from the saddle. He was tired already with the day not half done and he knew the bay mare needed rest, too. Sweat foamed on her flanks under the hot August sun and she yanked at the reins, wanting water and the shade of the cottonwoods along the river bank. He took the bit from her mouth and let her loose. She wouldn't go far. The road they'd traveled branched just ahead, crossing the river at a shallow ford to the south with the main track continuing west. And from that western direction he heard the grind of wagon wheels on rock.

A mismatched team came out of the cedars—a white shaggy pony and a sorrel mule. In the seat a one-armed man held the reins loosely and stared ahead, the left sleeve of his shirt pinned at the shoulder. Beside him a younger woman, her face half hidden from view by her sunbonnet, returned Hub's wave. They crossed the ford, water falling off the wheels and off the legs of the team like shards of a broken mirror and continued up the slow-rising hill on the other side.

The mare found a thick stand of grass. Hub stretched down on his belly at the water's edge and as he drank he smelled the wet current and the dark leaves of other summers. He found a round boulder beneath the limbs of a cypress and let the wind cool the sweat out of his hair. A fish slapped the water downriver. The midday air smelled of scorched limestone and torn grass. He leaned back and closed his eyes and let his thoughts lose focus. The grazing horse ate at the grass with sounds like the distant firing of skirmish lines. Funny he'd never noticed that before. No matter how many years went by, and it was eight or nine now, something was always reminding him of the war, the way it sounded or smelled, or felt.

Wasteful thing it was, too. Wasteful and dirty and heartbreaking.

His three-day ride had brought him from the banks of the muddy Brazos through black farmland where men worked at excising the trees of the countryside, through Austin, where the Republicans worried over the laws of the land, then along the Colorado and Pedernales into this higher place with its hills of limestone, clear water and trees that struggled for their life, twisting their way into sunlight through whatever cracks the rocks allowed them. A clean, stark beauty. But it was said to attract dark-hearted people.

From the tumbled hills and valleys of the Llano outlaw bands raided gentler landscapes and returned to hide in the dense cedar brakes and limestone caves along the sweet water of the river and its tributaries, but no matter, that wasn't Hub's concern. He had come with different interests. So far nobody had bothered him, and if it stayed that way he'd keep his pistol in the saddlebag and his Winchester in its scabbard.

The mare was nervous coming up from the ford into the beginnings of the new settlement. The smell of fresh-cut wood reached Hub from a half-dozen piles of logs and lumber and canvas on the high ground between the north and south forks of the Llano. There was dust in the air, and voices, the smell of wood smoke, cooking food, and garbage. Hot sun on the backs of everything. A small group of men stood outside the only saloon, their laughter loud and unwelcome in his ears. There was always a saloon and there were always men who lived their lives in its shadow. No doubts about the log structure across the way, the word *Jail* carved over the door. Elsewhere the pounding of hammers and the slow emergence of what would someday be a town. If another flood didn't get it.

The wagon team he'd seen earlier stood at the hitch rail of the *Kimbleville Store,* switching their tails at flies. Two Mexicans wearing sombreros leaned their backs against the one-room building. Made of notched logs that had lost their color and warped from the heat, with a tin roof turning rusty-red in places, the store had been there a while. Its sign was made of short lengths of cedar branches nailed to a board and hung beside the open door.

He tied the mare and went inside, bending a little to clear the jamb and looked around the room. Not much merchandise; a few barrels of food staples–beans, flour, coffee–a counter that held three or four bolts of cloth, some tools and steel traps hanging from pegs, two rifles on the wall behind the counter where James Harper stood. Harper glanced at him as he entered, then continued his conversation with the man and woman from the wagon. Another fellow with sawdust in his hair stood next to the tools. It was cooler in here but still hot. Summer's heavy hand seemed to muffle voices and colors. Flies droned in and out of the doorway.

James had grown that black beard, and Hub wouldn't have known him if he'd seen him anywhere else. Last time was over on the Louisiana line in the Red River fighting, leg blown half off, riding in the cart with the other wounded, white with shock and on his way to a certain amputation and a possible death. Never able to learn James' fate, he had mourned his friend until a letter came one day, and so one thing at least the war had not taken from him.

"Hubbard Anderson?" James was staring at him. The others heard the surprise and looked at him with curious faces.

"Howdy, James." He lifted his hat in acknowledgement.

"My god." Harper raised a hinged section of the countertop and reached for him in an awkward shuffle, dragging the stiff limb.

Hub said, "Still can't believe you don't have a peg leg."

"Came close enough," Harper said with a short laugh and a glance down. "I resorted to threats that involved firearms and held 'em at bay until they changed their minds. At the time I thought I'd rather die than live as a one-legged man." He patted Hub's shoulders. "It's a position I have since rethought."

To the man and woman he said, "Ben, Sarah, this here's my old tent mate you've heard me talk about, Hubbard Anderson. These are the Turners, Hub. Father and daughter—I'll let you pick out which is which, and over there's Joe Biggs, a man of the carpentry trade." The man with sawdust in his hair smiled and mumbled something and went back to his study of tools.

The laughter from near the saloon turned louder, poking through the door like dirty fingers. The Turner woman went past them and stood watching out the door, then screamed "Johnny!" and left at a run.

"I had better see about this, Hub." James got a walking cane, and Hub stayed beside him across the street. The older man remained inside. Joe Biggs came along slowly, interested but cautious.

CHAPTER 2

A fist fight was going on. Between the spectators Hub could see arms flailing. One of the fighters went down. The other one held a club of some kind. It rose in the air and descended. Sarah Turner had circled the roil of men, trying to get inside them, screaming the name again. In front of him James tried to get through and failed, someone's elbow blocking him. Hub caught hold of the arm and shoved the man aside to make room. The elbow swinger averted his eyes and stepped aside and James lurched ahead. In the center stood a man with the look of a work horse gone to fat. His face was red with heat and alcohol. James raised the cane as if to threaten him and said, "Stop this right now, Manning."

Manning planted a foot on the bad knee and shoved James back into Hub. James groaned. Sarah burst through on the other side and knelt beside the unconscious man–boy, really, maybe seventeen, eighteen years old–and began to wipe his face with her hand. An empty whiskey bottle lay in the dust beside him.

She looked up at the big man and said, "He's drunk. Don't hurt him any more."

Hub was aware of golden hair and blue eyes full of tears. Manning raised the club again as though to strike her or the boy, then brought it down by his side.

"Go on, squaw. Take the halfbreed with you." A badge was pinned on the man's dirty shirt. Ben Turner had come up beside Hub. He looked around now with hurt on his face and the sag of futility in his shoulders.

Hub decided somebody ought to put a stop to this. He took two steps and was close enough to Manning to smell foul breath and see the black pores in his skin, feel the hate radiating off him. Flat eyes fastened on Hub. "What? I got to whip you next?"

The noise around them dropped in anticipation. Hub heard a single female voice from somewhere in the crowd say *squaw* in a conversational tone, as though it carried no malice. A horse whinnied in the distance, a redwing dove flew close and circled away in a clatter of wings.

He swung his open right hand from near his hip pocket in a rising arc that caught the side of Manning's head, ricocheting up and out like a cannon shot. Manning went down hard into the arms of men who could have caught him but merely stepped aside and let him fall. Manning pulled a pistol as he fell.

"This man is unarmed!" James shouted, but it didn't stop the draw. Hub had seen it happening in time to move to one side as the barrel lifted toward him, and he planted the sharp toe of a boot into the gunhand. The crack of bone, a yell of pained surprise and the gun spun away.

Just then another voice cut through the crowd. "That's enough, men. Get along now, everybody go on." Manning struggled to his feet, shame and murder on his face. The voice belonged to a smaller man, clean-shaven and well-dressed in a suit and necktie, a badge on his coat lapel, the look of authority about him, and something else–challenge and the nearly hidden wish to harm. He stopped in front of Hub. "You're under arrest."

James protested, "Captain, that ain't right. This man of yours..."

"I said that's enough, Mr. Harper. Help these people get the drunkard boy off the street." James sucked in a heavy breath, but said nothing more and began to help Sarah lift the boy and prepare to carry him to the wagon. The carpenter Joe Biggs helped them. Ben Turner watched. The woman brushed dirt off her clothing and ran her hands through her hair and looked at the circle of faces with undisguised contempt.

"You're cowards, all of you," she said. "Let me tell you a secret. This boy is the son of Two Hawks. And I...I was the wife of Two Hawks. If my husband were alive he would cut out your hearts for this. And worse things than that." She met the eyes of everyone there as if memorizing their presence. Even James seemed to be taken aback by what she'd said. In the silence, her back straight and her face composed she walked through them. They carried the boy after her. The captain pulled a pair of handcuffs from his coat pocket and fitted them on Hub's wrists. He pointed to the jail.

The two men in sombreros mounted horses and rode away.

CHAPTER 3

Hub sat on the edge of the cot in the hot, uncomfortable room, letting time pass until the next thing happened, whatever it might be. Calm acceptance had become part of his makeup years before when he began learning about dark-hearted people.

He hoped James would care for his mare until they turned him loose. But who were *they?* The badge on the captain's coat looked official, but not quite like any he'd ever seen. After an hour the door to the front opened and heavy steps approached down the short hallway. In a moment the six-inch hole sawn in the upper portion of Hub's door framed Manning's face. He said, "You ought not to done that. Next time you won't get no sucker punch on me."

Hub lay back on the cot, his arms behind his head. "It wasn't."

"What do you mean?"

"It was not a punch. I slapped you. Openhanded."

Manning stared in, seemed confused, started to speak again, seemed to think better of it and walked away. Hub let out a sigh. It would take more than words with than one. Whatever the source of the big man's enmity, it was focused on him now and would have to play itself out. That was okay, but it was wearisome, too.

He must have slept. Light slanted through the tiny window from a different direction. Another stranger stood at the open door. This one was younger than the others. A broken tooth left a gap in his mouth, and he, too, wore that badge. He said, "Stand up. Get your hat."

Hub's left arm tingled from lack of circulation. He rubbed it and said, "What is that? The badge?"

"Why, it's the State Police badge."

"That right? Well you boys are mighty hard on women and kids, aren't you?"

The young man glanced behind as if someone might overhear. "Leo's the only one done that. The captain don't go along with such..."

"Bring him up here, Cooter! I'm waiting on you!"

"Yes, sir," he called back, motioning for Hub to follow.

James was there with a careful smile. Behind the desk was the captain, trim of body, bald, waiting like an impatient predator. "Stand before the desk, sir." He examined papers for a few silent moments and said, "Anderson, is it? Well, Mr. Anderson, your friend here has told me a little about you and paid your fine of twenty dollars. I'm going to set you free with the understanding that you'll mind your manners better while you're here. You agree to that?"

"I expected to go before a judge, sir, tell my side of the story."

"No judge, friend, no story. My decision *is* the law, as you will discover if you create any further disturbance." He nodded with a curt dip of his head and said, "You are dismissed."

They took it slow walking back to the store, allowing for Harper's stiff leg. "I don't understand what happened back there, James. What kind of law is that?"

James breathed hard with the effort. "I didn't have time to warn you, with all that happened after you showed up. Likely you've heard about the police force the Republicans set up. I don't know about elsewhere, but it's been a disaster out here.

Governor Davis sent Dugan to put down the outlaws that hide in the rough country hereabouts and he's turned out to be worse than any of them. That fine I just paid? Goes in his pocket. Taxes, fees, everything."

"You ought to complain to the governor then."

"Don't you think we've tried? But Davis will be kicked out of office soon, and there's talk of disbanding this force and bringing back the Rangers. Things are about to change for the better, I can feel it."

The ride home was a silent one. Neither Sarah nor her father wanted to talk. The boy lay in the wagon bed just as they'd placed him, unmoving. Sarah checked his breathing from time to time and he seemed to be all right except for the bruise on his head where Manning had connected with the club. This was not the first time they'd carried John Turner home drunk, sick, filthy with his own vomit. But it was different this time. After all these years of hiding the truth, how could she have been so foolish? A rush of anger and hurt, and the opening of old wounds.

She and her son would be treated even worse now. Just look—her own father sitting there encased in his outrage like a fist of flint. What had she done?

They washed the boy as best they could at the horse trough and got him inside the house and in bed. Benjamin Turner left to put away the team. She heard the screen door slam shut as she gathered Johnny's foul clothing and carried it outside to the washpot. Against the harsh sun beginning its descent to night Ben led the wagon team and the boy's paint toward the pasture, holding all their reins in his one hand, his pinned left sleeve waving in the hot wind like the useless wing of a doomed bird.

She lit a lamp, built a fire in the stove and made a simple supper, set the kitchen table for two. And waited. Dark settled over the house like a brooding hen and still he didn't return. Well, it had to be talked about. The secret had hung inside her like a bat in a dark cave, always poised to fly, and now it had flown and broken her heart again. Johnny was sleeping, his face at peace now. He wouldn't wake til morning, and he would be better then. She carried the lamp with her.

There was no light at the barn, but that's where he would be. It's where he always went when disappointment and confusion got too heavy. Talked to his wife's ghost. Remembered. Her lamp threw shadows in a gray dance along the wall and among the harness and bridles hanging there. He sat in his cowhide chair leaning back against a post, hat in his lap.

"Your supper's ready." He didn't answer. Didn't look at her. A nightbird sang in the woods outside. The barn was filled with the loamy, thick smell of hay. Sarah held the lamp and refused to leave. "I'm sorry, papa." It seemed to her just then that they had always posed like this—each wishing to change what could never be changed and shadows all around.

"You like to know where I was when the Indians took you?" His eyes were on something distant.

"Buying cattle, you always said."

"Well, I lied about that. I was carousing in San Antonio. Drunk." He looked at her then, the lamp flame reflecting off his eyes. "I come home to find your mama killed, you gone, the place half burned down, stock run off. Feeling about like Johnny's going to feel tomorrow. I never touched whiskey again, but it was already too late to matter."

"You couldn't have stopped the things that happened."

"No, but I could have died beside my wife." *More secrets,* Sarah thought. He went on; "Why'd you say that back in town? It wasn't his bunch stole you."

"It was another Comanche band that took me, but they traded me to him."

"So it's the truth, then. You and me's swapped lies all these years."

"I was afraid if I told you, told other people Two Hawks was Johnny's father they'd want to kill him, everyone hated Two Hawks so. And I didn't really mean to tell it today, either. It was just something that said itself, with me listening."

"Ah, Sarah, nobody much cares anymore. Nobody remembers, except me and you. People just like to look down on somebody else, and you and your boy was handy. It's always seemed strange to me you wouldn't know the name of the man who got you with child."

"Well, now you know. And in the morning I'll tell Johnny."

"May be a good thing for him. It could make a difference, all this time thinking he was the child of some buck or other without a face or a name. That Two Hawks was a terror to us out here, but he was a fine war chief to his people and as brave a man as I ever saw. The boy can be proud of that."

"His father was a great warrior, and I loved him very much."

Ben turned his head away as if her words were stones. "God blessed me that day we found you alive and well. Lost my arm out there, but it was a trade I was glad to make to have you back again."

It occurred when she was four years old. At first she thought she was still dreaming when she woke with a stinking hand so tight across her mouth and nose she could hardly breathe. A vaguely remembered ride that lasted days. A more sharply remembered fear and a longing that lasted a much greater time until it merged with happier feelings. A picture in which she was part of another family. Their language was different, but it became hers. A father, a mother. When the soldiers left them alone their life was a happy one. It would hurt Ben Turner to know she missed those people to this very day. By the time she entered adolescence and the war chief sought her as wife she could imagine no other life.

She was his second wife, the other an older woman who cared for her much as a mother might. For three summers she did not share her husband's blanket. When she was older she became pregnant and that was a very pleasant time in their lodge. There was more meat than they needed, and they shared it with others, plenty of skins for clothing and moccasins. No one could want more.

16

Sometimes the warriors went away for a time, led by her husband, and they would return with horses and sometimes scalps of the enemy. It never occurred to her that Ben Turner was one of their enemies. She had forgotten.

That winter was the coldest anyone could remember and the band moved south. They meant to go into Mexico where the weather would be warmer and the old people and children would not be sick from the cold. One day they camped on the Llano, not far from the Turner ranch. She had no memory of the country, had thoughts only of her baby's coming birth, and it was in that camp that he was born. Two Hawks delayed moving while she rested from her labor. She was very young and it had been difficult.

The delay cost everything.

They were seen by a hunting party and next morning a troop of mounted men thundered through the camp, firing their guns until the people were either dead or hiding in the woods. When the men found her and the baby concealed beneath a buffalo robe she thought they would kill her, too, but instead they were gentle. She was brought before a badly wounded man who stared into her face with eyes glazed over by pain. His clothing was covered with blood and she believed he must be dying. He tried to reach for her, but lost consciousness, and the men took her away.

It was a long time before the English language began returning to her, and then it flowed like something remembered rather than learned, and she was careful to lie because she was sure the white men would kill the baby if they found out who he was.

"All this time I've acted toward you and Johnny like I'm the one who's important, like it's *my* feelings that matter, not yours."

She offered him a kindness. "You've given us a home."

"*Given?* Why Sarah, this *is* your home. No, I've been selfish with my love. You know that. But today—what's tearing me up inside right now is knowing the truth about something I've

17

always wondered about. Why it was that Two Hawks fought us so hard that day. He give up his life, Sarah. He died trying to..." Ben's voice snagged on something. It was a minute before he could finish. "He was trying to save his wife and son. And we killed him for it."

The pain in his voice pulled her closer. He fumbled to his feet and put his arm around her waist and her head fell against his shoulder.

He stroked her hair as if she were still the child he lost once. "What was your name then? What did Two Hawks call you?"

"Sun Woman. He called me Sun Woman."

"Because of your hair."

"Yes."

They went in the house and had their supper and talked far past midnight, each of them aware that love comes in many disguises.

CHAPTER 4

The town had no livery stable but they'd built a corral for horses down the hillside behind Harper's store, made it of brush and limestone rocks, one corner of it on a spring of water that filled a pool and ran down to the river. Hub spared his friend's leg and carried a half sack of oats and two nosebags to his mare and the only appaloosa in the bunch, a gelding that belonged to James.

He sat on a portion of rock wall and watched them eat, the other horses crowding around them wanting a share of the food. It was almost dark and James was making some supper in the leanto at the back of the store that was his bedroom and kitchen.

It seemed to Hub a long time since he'd ridden in and he was tired. A dog barked somewhere, now and then a note from the piano inside the saloon drifted past like a sparrow separated from its flock. It didn't take long for the animals to finish their rations. He collected the bags and remaining oats and climbed the hill. He'd forced James to take twenty dollars, of course, to cover the fine, though he'd had to insist on it. Still, he hadn't brought much money with him and he had even less now and who knew what expenses he would run into before he got done with his business.

His *business*. He laughed silently at himself. Made it sound like he had a plan, when he had in fact nothing much but hope. Ever since the war ended and reconstruction set in, it seemed like there was a hand out for money everywhere you turned and a gun to back it up. Like that Dugan fellow up there with nobody to take him down. Never mind, though. He couldn't afford to get distracted. In the letters they'd exchanged James had told him about the outlaws, and about the herds of cattle roaming loose for any man's loop. Well, now *he* was the man with the loop and with luck he'd take a few head back to the Brazos, make another trip next summer, get his own herd started again.

Their homestead had been a good place before the war. Hard work for the two parents, his brother, himself, but Indians no longer raided there and it was rich land.

Sort of a joke that they'd never owned a slave, but had to fight for men who did, his brother and he. Lynn died at Gettysburg for some reason or other he'd never figured out. Because somebody ordered him to, of course, but that didn't seem like a good enough reason. As far away as it had been, the bullet that took Lynn took the parents as well, piercing their hearts with wounds that leaked their lives away, and nothing left when he returned except bare ground and the taxes and the echoes of his solitary mourning.

Supper was chili and biscuits cooked on a potbellied stove that heated the little room beyond endurance. They took their plates outside and ate standing at the hitchrail. James said between bites, "I'll have to ride out to the Turner ranch tomorrow. I'd like you to come along with me if you got the time."

The chili was good, filled with chunks of beef and hot peppers that bit back. "Is she the lady you wrote me about?" They'd had no time to talk about the happenings of the afternoon. Customers were in the store, and James hadn't seemed anxious to talk anyway.

"Yes, that was Sarah. They didn't get the supplies they came in for, so I thought the two of us could carry the stuff out there. Most of it, anyway."

Hub swallowed a spoonful of chili. "That's my direction James, judging from the way they came in. If you won't mind me riding on from there to rope some cows."

"Ben used to be the biggest rancher around here. Back before the Comanches stole Sarah and killed his wife. He's been drifting along ever since, but he could give you some good advice about where to look for cattle."

"That'd be welcome. I'm a pure stranger here and glad of any help I can get."

"Well, we're obliged to you for stepping in like you did. Lucky for them and me you appeared today." He ate the last out of his bowl. "I guess you're wondering about what Sarah said, about that Indian, Two Hawks. Ever heard that name?"

"No, James, I never did."

"Well, you're from a different part of the country. He was a war chief of the tribe, lots of stories about him, mostly bad ones. It was his band that Ben and a bunch of others rescued Sarah from. They killed him in the fight–most of his people, too. Sarah had the baby with her when she was found and has tried to raise him among whites that act mostly like you saw today. She'd never said who the daddy was, so you could say it was a surprise."

"The boy get drunk like that before?"

"Yes, sad to say. He's played the part of the drunken halfbreed for three or four years now. Ben about quit having anything to do with him."

Hub said, "Whiskey can get a powerful hold on some people, Indians in particular. He's young, though. Maybe he's not a lost cause just yet."

"I hope not, for Sarah's sake."

"You plan to marry her?" He was sorry for the question the second he'd asked it. None of his business, but James wasn't offended, smiled in fact.

"When she'll have me."

"Her boy could make life rough on everybody."

"He could. Probably will. But she's worth it, Hub. I've waited a long time. What about you? Making any plans like that?"

"No sir, and don't expect to. There's always work out in front of me and no time for anything else." He finished the chili and ate the last of a biscuit.

They heated water and filled a galvanized tub with it and Hub washed off three days of dust and sweat. Compared to their days together in the Confederate Cavalry this was rare luxury and a fine way to end the day. He spread his bedroll on the floor and went to sleep watching the flicker of dying coals in the little potbellied stove.

———————

The boy woke before daylight with the familiar sense of dread. The room was cool and he pulled his blanket up with fingers that trembled. The small movement caused nausea and a knife-like slice of pain behind his eyes. Dawn couldn't be far. Already a rooster crowed in the coop behind his grandfather's barn. Faint odors of woodsmoke and coffee reached him and he knew his mother was awake and in the kitchen and the old man already moving around, checking the hens, the horses, watching for the sunrise.

What would this day hold for him?

Recriminations, of course, her tears and Benjamin Turner's threats. Or his silence, which was worse. John's place in this house, at the Turner table, had always seemed temporary, as though he could lose it at any moment with a word, a look, the falling of a leaf. But the world outside–across the river, down long roads leading elsewhere–didn't want him, either. They whispered *halfbreed* and gave him whiskey.

Yesterday when he'd ridden into town before the wagon and the big policeman had called him over and offered a drink he should have turned it down and walked away. But he couldn't.

22

He was too weak, wanted it too much. There was danger in the faces of the idle men, but he drank with them anyway. The rest was like a dream–distorted images, movement without form. Pain.

The latch on his door scraped and soft fabric brushed against the rough wood. He wished she wouldn't come so soon. The bedspring squeaked as she sat on the edge of the bed. He was careful with his breathing, pretending sleep, wanting her to spare him a little longer.

But her hand smoothed his hair back from his face, touched a place that caused the pain behind his eyes again and a movement of his head.

"You awake, Johnny?"

His mouth was dry, his tongue thick and slow. "I'm sorry, mother."

A tear hit his cheek. "Oh, Johnny, I have done you a terrible wrong."

CHAPTER 5

A whitetail doe came into the trail ahead and stopped to stare round-eyed at them. James tugged his mount to a stop and whispered, "Shoot her." Hub slid his Winchester from its scabbard and raised it just as a fawn followed. For a second he strained with intent and then lowered the rifle.

The Turners were low on supplies and two more hungry men at their table might work a hardship. The doe would be fine venison, but Hub only shook his head and settled the rifle across the pommel of his saddle. "Let's wait for a buck."
At the sound of his voice the doe and fawn sprang into the trees, tails raised like flags of surrender.

"A buck will make stringy eating," James said without heat. No man ever shot straighter than this red-haired Texan beside him. Or quicker. In battle he'd been a fearsome soldier who seldom missed his mark. Now this. Would you call it gentleness? Maybe, but it lived in a man who could lay a three-hundred pound bully in the dirt with his open hand.

The hills were full of deer, and a few minutes later they did jump a buck, a four-pointer resting in grass beside the trail and Hub brought him down in the midst of his first leap. They dressed him out beside a clear spring of water in a close-by cedar brake, the raw odors of the deer mingling with the softer scents of cedar and new water. A raven waited in a Spanish Oak and three buzzards circled overhead when they rode away, the carcass strapped behind Hub's saddle, the bay mare twisting her neck to see the unfamiliar burden on her back.

A long-eared hound met them as they rode past the house to a tree in back where they hung the buck. Sarah Turner stood in the open door waiting for them. When they'd unloaded the sacks of supplies from the horses she allowed James to hug her and said over his shoulder to Hub, "We're grateful for what you did yesterday."

In the kitchen she took two cups down from a shelf and said, "There's coffee left over from breakfast." She sat them at an ornately carved table in another room. "My mother brought this up from Galveston before I was born. I think she must have missed pretty things." The coffee was stale but neither man minded. A small and common occurrence that had long ago ceased to matter.

Sarah left them alone for a few minutes and returned with the boy following. His face was bruised and a knot stood on his forehead. He avoided their eyes. She sent him to take care of the two horses and to find Benjamin with news of company.

A dozen questions troubled James Harper, but this wasn't the time. He told her about Hub and their friendship in the war, and about the time they'd helped to swing a ruined ship crossways in the Red River to block Union boats, and about the banner they'd hung on it inviting the yankees to a ball in Shreveport. And about the steady decimation of E Company.

He did not talk about Hub's plans to round up stray cattle. It wasn't his place to discuss another's hopes and plans still tender and aborning. There was attention in her eyes, but behind it a sadness.

No woman James had ever known was such a mix of beauty and intelligence, of patience and gentleness and every other virtue that touches a man and causes him to hurt with desire. An understanding had grown up between them since his return.

They didn't discuss the future, and he had always realized his feelings were stronger than hers, but he'd meant it when he'd told Hub the night before that he'd wait as long as it took

Bothersome memories seemed to affect her still, and she spoke with a slight accent though she was adept and well-spoken in the English language, due he believed to the walls of books her mother had long ago brought to the Llano.

When Ben Turner entered the house he seemed a taller man than yesterday, standing straight, his hair iron-gray against the tan of his face. They stood to shake his hand and he joined them at the table. "Johnny wanted to cut up the venison," he said. "He's feeling shy, wants to be by his self."

Harper said, "Might be better if he stayed away from town a while. That Manning is a rough character."

Sarah moved a spoon from hand to hand, started to speak and then cleared her throat and began again.. "James, I know you're wondering about what I said, and I know you're waiting for a polite moment to ask about it, but we're not going to find a polite moment, or a polite way to talk about it. What I told was the truth, and if you want to hear the rest of it I'll tell you now."

Hub moved his chair back. "I've been watching your boy through the window, and that deer's too heavy for him. Think I'll go help him out."

Ben stood up as well. "I'll go with you, let these two have some privacy."

James *did* want privacy with this woman, but he saw at once that it was not going to be an easy or romantic time. She paced the floor, graceful and tense. "I told Johnny this morning," she said, "woke him up to do it, because I opened up Pandora's Box yesterday with him unconscious on the ground, and I couldn't bear it if some evil tongue brought the story to him all twisted out of shape. And for you, who have been my dearest friend, I want to do the same."

He listened without interrupting her, and understood at last what he had sensed for years–always hesitation, a certain distance. So it was only fear, then, fear that too much closeness would lead to discovery. When she finished he put his arms around her, ignoring her tiny, backward step, and pulled her close. "I love you more than ever, Sarah." The dread he'd felt last night, the nervousness on the ride out, had turned to gladness, and it seemed now he could hope to begin the life with her he had wanted for such a long time. "Thank you, James," she said.

Ben Turner watched Hub and the boy hang pieces of the butchered deer in the smokehouse. Its walls were browned from years of use. How many times had he come here to retrieve a haunch of beef or venison, a heavy ham for his wife's table? He built a tiny fire and they shut the door and then drew a bucket of water from the well and washed themselves. Johnny carried a pan of steaks inside and came out again. Ben said, "There's rockers yonder on the gallery." The boy stayed with them, and Ben guessed he wanted to talk but was put off by the stranger's presence.

A strong breeze blew up the hill, full of cedar and limestone and the pleasant, bitter smell of leaf and acorn. "We'll sit down to dinner pretty soon now I reckon." He wondered if his daughter and the Harper fellow would make a decision to marry. When that happened it might leave him alone and lonely on this place, but it would be better for her to have a normal life if she could find it.

"Out here on a visit are you, Mr. Anderson?" The question seemed to Ben the least intrusive manner of starting a conversation. The breeze settled for a moment and he caught the smell of browning meat from the kitchen. He wasn't often hungry, but today was different.

"Yes, sir. That, and I want to try collecting some of y'all's wild cattle and drive 'em back home."

"You don't say. Now, that's interesting. Just today I was thinking about that very same thing myself." The old hound began barking somewhere back near the barn. John Turner rose from his chair and began to walk away. "You don't have to leave, Johnny." He felt negligent, not giving the boy a better chance to talk to him. It was a talk they both needed.

"I'll see what he's barking at. Probably a fox after eggs." There was no spring in his walk. The liquor hadn't burned out of him yet. Ben turned back to his guest.

"Sorry, Mr. Anderson. Go on."

"Well, I've got some land back on the Brazos and I want to devote it to cattle, but I have no cattle, and frankly no money to buy them. I've heard there's plenty in this part of the state free for the taking–animals that wandered off from spreads during the war and went wild. I came out to see for myself."

"Oh, they're here, all right. I'll tell you that right now. Lot of 'em used to belong to me."

"I won't bother anything with a brand on it, Mr. Turner."

"Well, my point is that I've sat back on my hindside and let my herds drift off my land. I still have five pretty good sections left. Once had many times that, but I sort of let that drift away, too. And of course all these blamed hairy outlaws in the cedar brakes have to eat, so they rustle what they want, and I've turned into a cattleman without cattle, like you. We're singing the same tune."

He sat back and closed his eyes and was quiet for a long time, as though he'd finished what he had to say. At last he raised his head. "How you plan to go about it?"

Hub shrugged his shoulders. "Find some cows and pitch camp and go to catching 'em. When I get enough to make a drive I'll push 'em home and come back for more."

"What about the owlhoots?"

"Live and let live, I reckon. They don't bother me I won't bother them."

Turner laughed. "They'll sure as heck bother you. You've got to pen the herd somewhere safe."

"And where would that be?"

"Right here."

Hub sat back. "You mean here on your ranch? You'd offer me that?"

28

"That and more, Mr. Anderson. We could help each other out. I've got thirty acres of pasture fenced with smooth wire about a half-mile west of the house–built it for the very thing we're talking about and then never used it.

"You can pen and brand what you catch and hold them right there til you have enough for a drive. What's more, you can put up in my bunkhouse if you want. There's six beds in there that nobody uses. You think about it. I can help you locate the herds and what we catch we split down the middle. Safe from outlaws and they won't be running off on you." He saw Hub's eyes go to the empty sleeve.

"And you don't have to worry on that account, neither. I can hold up my side of the bargain, and it ain't likely you can do it alone." He stood up and adjusted the waist of his trousers. "You don't have to decide this minute, anyhow. Think about it while we eat some of that good venison you brought and maybe we can talk some more later."

Hub stood, as well. "Mr. Turner..."

"Let's us call each other by first names."

"All right. Ben...you need my help, too, is that right? I mean, it's not just for me. Am I right about that?"

"I thought I just said so."

"No offense meant. I just want to know that you'd get a fair return on the deal."

"Mr....Hub, I was there yesterday, and I've watched you today and heard the way you talk, and I believe I can tell some things about you. I don't have a doubt in the world you'll give me more than my share."

Sarah called them to eat.

"If that's the case, well, then I don't need to think about it. I reckon I'll take you up on the offer, and much obliged to you." They shook on it and headed inside. What Ben didn't say was that he hoped John would help out, too. Spend time with this man, learn from him, but that wasn't something you could push. It would happen or not, and they would have to wait and see.

There was fried venison on the table, a platter of biscuits and a bowl of gravy along with greens from Sarah's garden. James seemed subdued and had little to say as they pulled up chairs.

"Where's Johnny?" Sarah asked.

"I thought he was in here," Ben answered. "Still down at the barn, I reckon. I'll go find him."

"No, you men start your meal. I'll go."

She walked to the barn, stopped along the way to pick a bluebonnet. Inside, the smell of hay and livestock met her as she entered. "Johnny?" No answer. The hound appeared, his tail looped between his hind legs, tight against his belly. She felt a sudden heavy dread in her chest, the flick of pulse in her throat. She walked outside, far enough to see the horses. All there, with their heads down grazing, including the boy's pinto.

She yelled "Johnny!" but heard no response and went back to the house with fear coiled inside her like a black snake.

CHAPTER 6

John Turner found the barking hound at the fringe of trees behind the barn, hair standing stiff on the old dog's neck as he peered into thick brush. John praised him, getting a wet tongue across his wrist. The hound did a fine job of keeping varmints out of the enclosure that provided minimal safety to Sarah's flock of hens.

He thought about the two men at the house, wished they would go back to town. Something good had happened this morning and he wanted to talk about it with Sarah and Ben. Sarah had seemed to expect bitterness from him when she woke him, but he'd felt none of that. Instead, there had been disbelief that slowly turned into stunning belief and a joy he had never felt before.

He was after all the son of a warrior chief and not some accidental thing that nobody really wanted. How could he keep quiet the jubilation in his heart?

The dog growled and John silenced him with a gesture and a word, and a moment later something came over his head and he was enveloped in darkness.

Powerful arms held him, a hand crushed the covering against his face so that he couldn't cry out for help. He heard a yelp of pain from the hound and he was lifted and carried, hearing only the sounds of feet in fallen leaves and the scratch of tree limbs. The thing around him stank with a raw, meaty stench. They stopped after minutes of travel and it was lifted off him–it was a buffalo robe–revealing two men dressed in the clothing of Mexican peasants.

The one who had carried him was older than the other one and more muscular. His hair was cut short around his ears like someone had held a bowl over the man's head and sheared around it.

"Friend," he said, pointing to himself and the younger man, who looked to be not much older than John. There seemed to be no threat about him, and John felt a tiny thrill of relief. "Friend," he said again. "Not hurt."

"What do you want?" John was embarrassed by the tremble in his own voice.

"You come." He motioned for John to mount one of the horses, but John began taking backward steps, preparing to run. The younger man closed the distance between them and caught him by the arm.

"You're crazy. I'm not going anywhere with you."

"You quiet." His face had turned harder and a little frightening. John obeyed.

The man got into his own saddle and pulled a rifle from its scabbard. John climbed up and the younger one vaulted onto the horse's rump behind him with almost no effort. They moved out at a trot, John full of silent questions, afraid he might never return.

They traveled for at least an hour, maybe more, crossing and recrossing creeks. Many times he thought of jumping from the moving horse, but unless he was very lucky the man with the rifle would stop him with bullets or words before he could get away.

By now they would miss him at home, were probably already looking for him. Had they killed old Jack? If the hound was alive he could trail them even though they'd laid out a confusing route. Finally they drew the horses to a halt amid a pile of granite boulders. The Llano was not far. He saw the flash of running water, smelled it in the heated wind. The young one whistled the call of a bobwhite quail and it was answered nearby.

A small group of people appeared, hesitant and watchful. Two women, one very old, bent like a rotting reed, the other younger, a girl. A very pretty girl. Another man stood straight, gray hair in long braids, face wrinkled with age. They all looked tired.

When John dismounted there was a scatter of conversation in a language not Spanish that seemed to focus on him. Eyes swung past him, pausing just seconds before traveling elsewhere. The old woman came close and took his face between hands that seemed small and sharp as the paws of a wild varmint. She smelled like woodsmoke and musk. Looked over his face, into his eyes, and seemed at last satisfied.

She laughed. Not with humor, but with a sound more like surprised discovery and turned to the others who waited and said something. The pretty girl regarded him with open curiosity, taut as an antelope testing the wind.

"Tu madre?" The woman's voice reminded him of the squeal off a wagon wheel.

"My mother?"

"Si." This made less sense to him all the time, but at least there was no animosity from them. He began to feel a little better.

"You know my mother?" She didn't answer, but motioned to the girl, who brought a gourd of water.

The men took seats in a circle. A long-stemmed pipe was produced and lit and the old man puffed at it, blowing smoke in four directions. He beckoned John with a gesture of his hand to sit at his side. The girl came up behind him and said, "I talk for them."

He tried to turn enough to see her face but could not. "Why did you bring me here?"

"Look front is better." Her voice was calm, as if she instructed him in some civilized decorum. It was difficult to contain his agitation.

The old man beside him put away the pipe and began talking in a sing-song voice, looking first at the sky then down at his feet. The talk seemed to carry anger, then sadness, then hope, and at the last of it there was a smile on the thin, hard lips when he became silent.

Over his shoulder John heard "This man say about you sit here."

"How come you speak English?"

"Somebody teach me. I talk for these." The others watched their conversation as if they understood the words. The old woman stood apart, leaning against a slab of rock and looking into the sky.

"You had no right to kidnap me, whatever you want."

"Ki...nap?" It did not come off her tongue smoothly.

"Steal me."

"You not steal. What more he say is you son of Two Hawks. Chief now."

"How do you know that?" He heard his own voice rise in disbelief. "I didn't know myself until this morning."

"The town. The woman say."

"You were there?"

"Father. Brother." She said, nodding toward the men who had brought him. "They come tell." He almost laughed aloud in reaction, but caught himself in time, knowing it would be an unwelcome or even dangerous response.

"Maybe it's a lie."

"No. This woman." She indicated the old one still standing quietly, still holding the water gourd as if ready to offer him another drink. "See you borning. Now she see Two Hawks your face." There was a burn in his eyes. He blinked it back, this new avalanche of feelings pouring down on him. Perhaps he was still asleep and dreaming. The hurt of whiskey had not worked its way completely out of his body yet. The knot on his

34

head throbbed. He was hungry. A deer fly lit on his hand, then launched again when he moved. What had she said about *chief*?

"Are you Comanches?"

"Same like you."

Not like me, he thought. You're all one thing and I'm half everything. "Is this all of you?"

"More people long ride this place."

"I thought all the Indians around here had gone on the reservation." She turned to the old man and spoke a few words and waited for his reply.

"He say you hunt buffalo some hide. We like that."

He looked around at the expectant faces. A handful of vagabonds who might be caught or killed any second, especially now that his grandfather was on their trail, and John had no doubt about that. He knew better than anyone that Ben Turner had no love for Indians.

Since Sarah had said those things this morning he'd felt dazed and elated through the hangover, strangely happy. But there was no happiness in this. This was futile, these people living in an illusion, hiding out, evading the capture that would surely come soon. There was nothing he could do for them, they had no right to expect it. He could not even take care of himself. The old despair curled in his gut. He shook his head, causing the circle of men to grunt as though clearing their throats.

"Tell them I'm just a boy, not a chief. I can't help you." A bullet trilled off the rock. He heard the flat crack of a distant rifle.

35

CHAPTER 7

John felt a needlelike spray of rock dust strike his face. More bullets, a gasp of pain from the girl as the others scattered and the old woman fell and lay still. He grabbed the girl and pulled her to the ground beside him. There was a red patch on her shoulder where the garment was torn open. Blood on his hand. Her muscles quivered with shock from the impact. This couldn't be his grandfather, there hadn't been time enough. But what kind of cold blooded...

Hooves drummed the rocky ground, invading his thoughts. Another shot ricocheted nearby. The ragged people had melted into hiding without a sound. No screams, no confusion. How quick they were, how silent. He pulled her into the shadow of an overhang, examined her shoulder. It was a grazing wound, not deep. She would be all right.

"There goes one!" Came a shout, then the boom of a rifle. The sounds grew fainter and he realized that whoever the shooters were they were chasing the fleeing Indians. He lifted his head above the surrounding rocks and saw dust and movement near the river.

He said to her, "Stay here. I'm going for a closer look."

"The grandmother?" She said.

"She is dead." He could add nothing to the statement, nor could he look into the sadness of the young eyes.

The girl reached into her clothing and handed him an object– a trade knife with a six-inch blade, the handle of laminated leather topped by a metal ball. He had seen others like it at the town store.

When he took it from her it felt as if it belonged in his hand. As if he had always held it and always felt such rage. The hangover was gone. And the hunger. Some strange new thing hummed along the muscles of his arms and back as he picked a route to the distant sounds of fighting.

There were three horsemen. They carried lever-action rifles and they threw rounds in indiscriminate directions. An occasional shot answered and they would prance their horses about, dodging the fire, but nothing touched them. The Comanches were hidden in another pile of boulders that reached into the water. The only possible escape for them was the river. At the first shots the Indian ponies had run away. Two of their tormentors had dismounted and were moving steadily ahead into the rocks, their horses tied side by side to the trunk of a twisted mesquite.

The third was still in the saddle–a huge man on a tall, powerful horse, firing his weapon and calling encouragement to the others. The hand that worked the lever and trigger of the rifle was wrapped in a white bandage. It was Manning, the one who had gotten him drunk and hurt him. If he could somehow get close enough to the man maybe he could dislodge him with a rock and go for him with the knife. The thought of planting his blade in the big chest felt almost like a fierce hunger for food, he wanted it so much at this moment, like nothing he had ever before desired.

A flicker of movement caught his attention, something near the river bank in the cover of tall grasses. A man crawled rapidly out of sight then reappeared near the two tethered horses. It was the one who had brought him here, the girl's father. He untied the horses and led them away while Manning fired into the rocks.

John began working down from his position, then saw the two horses again, riderless, running straight for the policeman. Manning stopped using his rifle and simply watched them come until something thrust from under the neck of the leading horse and gunfire sounded. Manning fell to the ground.

The young Comanche came upright on the back of the other galloping pony and brought it to a halt, leaping down to take the fallen man's rifle. More bullets split the air from the two troopers in the rocks now, but they were aimed elsewhere, the men pinned between the old warrior above and the two below and there was nowhere they could hide. He heard one of them yell.

"We quit!" But the Indians paid no attention, advancing rapidly and firing as they went. He heard another yell, this time a scream of pain and all at once there was no sound at all.

He ran to the place where Manning lay on his back. Blood stained the front of his shirt. His eyes were open, the eyes of a wounded animal, and he was breathing but otherwise still. The eyes changed, focused on John with recognition as he approached. The man was alive, but for how long? John knelt and put the blade of his knife against the hated throat. One thrust and he could bleed himself of shame and anger while he watched Manning's life pour out.

"You just killed an old lady," he said. "Why?" There was no response. He rose up. The man could die or not, it wasn't his concern. He continued on into the boulders and found the three Comanche men clustered near the bodies of the dead police. The old man had been wounded in one of his legs and they were tending him. John felt sick to his stomach.

What had they done?

These killings would cause terrible retribution. Nobody would care what caused it. It would never be seen as self-defense, or an act of war. These people would be slaughtered as murderers, and maybe that was his fate as well. Benjamin Turner would be among the slaughterers again, ready to kill anyone with red skin.

Where was his place in all of this? Moments ago he had almost slit Manning's throat. The other two who died? Well, they'd been willing to kill innocents, had done so. A harmless old woman lay dead just a few yards away, this man wounded in front of him, and the young girl with her bleeding arm. They had come after the Indians like sport.

He no longer wished to waste his heart on such men.

The dog was running in circles, nose to the ground, trying to pick up the scent again. Hub rode out of the thick woods that bordered the creek. Behind him came Sarah, riding her son's pony, the others far behind them now, Harper's stiff leg hanging on branches and saplings, slowing him down, and Ben Turner no telling where, trying to ride the mule, the only mount available to him when they'd hurriedly started the chase.

There was no time to hang back waiting for them if he wanted to keep the hound in sight so Hub fought his way through the slapping, slashing thickness as fast as his mare could travel, and always close behind was the pinto, Sarah grimly silent, one arm raised in self-protection.

Their horses' breathing was harsh and quick as they paused to watch the hound. "They've gone in the water," Hub said after a moment. "Likely ride up a ways and come out again." He touched the mare's flank with a boot heel. "I'll ride up that side of the creek and you take this one. Keep the dog with you." Sarah followed his instructions without comment.

There were two horses, one of them carrying more weight than the other. And they were traveling fast. Had they kidnapped the boy, or was he going with them willingly? One thing certain–this was interfering with Hub's plans to round up cattle. If the boy had gone off on a lark he would have some things to say to him, all right.

Whoever the riders were, they knew how to lose trackers, and there wasn't a lot of daylight left, shadows already getting longer as the sun moved toward the horizon directly in front of them. For Hub the world became a close, hot eternity of cedar needles and hardwood saplings grown so tightly together it soon became impossible for the mare to push through it and he realized no one could have come this way.

He made his way back across the stream and rejoined Sarah. A half mile farther on the hound bayed and took off at a run, nose down and tail in the air. They escalated to a trot. Lucky to have the dog along. In this rocky landscape there were few tracks to follow.

A series of rifle shots sounded far in the distance, muffled and tattered by hills and trees. Sarah looked at him and he responded with a nod.

"Gunfire. Good ways ahead." She was off at a gallop. "Sarah, wait...!"

The woman was bent low over the neck of the pinto pony and paid no attention to his call. Reluctantly he followed, knowing they were putting too much strain on the horses, but understanding her fear and panic and her need to know. He caught up to her and rode in front, pulling the mare into a trot and forcing Sarah to a slower pace.

"Get out of my way! Johnny may be hurt!" Fear for the boy made her voice shrill and biting.

"You've got to slow down, Sarah. Wear out these horses and we'll be helpless."

"All right, but go. Just go!"

They rode in the direction of the shots. He calculated maybe an hour to get there, depending on the country. And the pace had to be kept slower or they were apt to kill the willing animals. He had no idea what might be happening to the boy, what they faced ahead. The sounds were tied to the youngster's disappearance, no doubt. But how?

Ben Turner wished for one of his usual mounts, but there hadn't been time. The sorrel mule was a fine work animal but not much of a ride. Its gait was rough and kept him off balance and unsure of his seat. *Maybe it's just as well,* he thought, watching James Harper thread his stiff, unyielding leg through the brush. Kept him back here with the other man without making a show of it. The trail was easy enough to follow–Hub and Sarah's passage had left broken foliage behind them and the hound's voice sounded from far ahead.

There'd been two horses. He had read that sign from the beginning. They came to the creek where Hub and Sarah had split, and just then heard the distant gunfire, very faint.

"Somebody shooting," Harper said.

Ben was suddenly afraid–not for himself, but for John and for Sarah who had no business up there. He had lost her once and couldn't bear it again. But when he'd ordered her to stay behind she'd ignored him, ignored everyone, intent and single-minded on the trail of the lost boy.

"I wish she'd stayed home," James said as they resumed the pace.

Ben smiled in spite of his fears. "Why didn't you make her do it?"

"Me make her? Why didn't you?" They rode close together, close enough to talk for the first time since they'd left.

"Your friend Anderson. Will he take care of her?"

No hesitation in James' reply, "You don't have to worry on that score."

"I didn't think so. Strikes me as a right straight feller." Harper didn't answer, intent on their progress, but Ben noticed a quick tightening around the man's lips and eyes, and read the meaning. Friends, yes, but Harper was jealous, too, not only because Hub was with Sarah, but because he was a whole man, with no ungainly leg to hold him back.

"I want to thank you for standing up for us back in town."

"I didn't exactly stand up. Went down pretty quick, in fact."

"No, sir! You listen here. You faced the man, James. And don't let me hear you say different. You're no less a man than your friend." He watched Harper's face relax a little, then goosed the mule's flank and got him up to a shambling trot.

They were a long time coming out of the thick growth into more open country, higher country, the beginnings of sunset

41

throwing rose-colored streaks behind the rising hills, and shadows growing darker. A cooler thread of wind burrowed through the day's heat, carrying musty smells of the coming night. They hadn't heard the dog for some time now. Birds had hushed against the changing day and Ben heard only the sounds of hooves on rocks and his own swift breathing as he brought the hard-gaited mule to a stop, rising in the stirrups for a clearer view. "See anything?" He said.

James didn't reply for a moment, then pointed downslope toward the river where something moved inside a wide shadow. "There," he said. Both men unsheathed carbines as they went ahead at an increased pace.

The pinto was there, grazing in tall grass, the white of its pattern showing first, and the bay mare, too, and then they were close enough to see figures standing beside a wall of rock. Ben called out, "Sarah?"

"We're here," she answered. "Come on in."

They stood beside a man who lay prone on the ground. A big man. Closer, it was Manning, the one who'd hurt the boy, unconscious or dead, his open shirt dark with blood. "Bad?" Ben stayed in the saddle. Harper dismounted.

"Bad enough." Hub's voice drifted up, strangely muffled in the deepening twilight. "Chest wound, but he could live through it." Sarah tore strips of cloth off the man's shirt and while Hub lifted the heavy torso she wrapped them around the upper chest and shoulder.

Ben left them, riding slowly over the ground, noting the many hoof marks left there, seeing the dark, rusty bloodstains on the rocks above, the prints of boots. And moccasins.

He rode back to the small group and climbed down, feeling the sting of age in his hips and back. "See anybody else?"

"Just him," Sarah said.

"You talk to him?" She shook her head sharply, still afraid, still worried for the boy; more worried now than before, with this new finding, and the blood.

"He was out when we found him," she said. "Wouldn't have

42

found him at all but for the dog and Hub's mare. She kept nosing down this direction til we finally came on and we saw him..." her voice trailed off in fatigue.

"Ben said, "Good thing I'm on that mule, I guess. These other ones couldn't carry him out. He weighs more'n the pinto pony."

"I don't care about him!" Sarah shot back "Where's my boy? What's happened to Johnny?" She was near collapse. Ben and James Harper started toward her at the same time, then Ben stepped back and let the younger man take her in his arms.

Hub said, "He's waking up."

The man's small, dark eyes focused slowly on the faces peering at him He stared at Sarah. "Your half-breed papoose," he whispered.

CHAPTER 8

John Turner liked the girl's arms around his waist. She rode on the saddle skirt close behind him and even in the discord of their haste he welcomed the touch. He guided the big horse of Manning toward the lowering sun. In single column the others ahead led them into and out of the creek crossings, taking the hardest, rockiest ground to elude pursuit. He had not asked where they were headed. In his thoughts he reached behind to his mother and grandfather and the life he knew, but this had turned bad now.

He should have killed Manning, of course, and then no one could be sure what happened. The man was an animal who didn't deserve to live, and yet John hadn't been able or willing to take the life. Had been weak. And because of his weakness these people would be hunted like coyotes. They traveled in silence except for the hard breathing of their horses, the chip of hoof on stone, the single cries of night birds.

Wasn't he as much a part of these people as those he'd left behind? Something in his blood knew them, and his heart reached out to them. In spite of all they'd endured the ragged ones carried themselves with bravery and dignity. But bravery would not be enough to save them. Their whole nation was penned now, their lands divided among the whites. What could they hope to accomplish by hiding and running? One more day of freedom, then one more, and on until the end. For their own good they should go onto the reservation. No one could be certain they were responsible for those men's deaths. Manning could identify only him. And that was what he'd say when they reached their destination tonight.

Hub filled in the last of the dirt and stood resting beside the shallow grave they'd dug with sticks and sharp stones. Harper and Sarah piled rocks on it to keep animals out. This would have to do. They had no way to carry the bodies with them.

Manning was mounted astride the mule, slumped into an odd shape, like molten lead poured out without a mold, fitting itself to gravity and contour at random. A new moon gave little light and they accomplished the last of their labors as much by feel as by sight.

Time for more decisions.

No one seemed to know what to say, and Hub left the others to decide. It was their home, their family involved. He was only passing through. It was Ben Turner who spoke up.

"I'll take him on back to the house. I can lead this old mule and walk it in a few hours. Can't leave him here. The rest of you can go on after John, if that's what you want."

Sarah said, "We can't see tracks now, it's too dark."

"Your dog'll follow them," Hub offered. "Dark won't affect his nose."

James Harper's voice–"It might be better if we all go back tonight, get a fresh start tomorrow. We still don't know who has the boy." Silence filled in around them as individual decisions were made.

"I can't," Sarah said.

"But listen," Harper began, "It's insane for you..."

"Just shut up! I don't answer to you, James. I have to know if Johnny's all right."

Her sharp retort hung in the air like a blade. There'd be no changing her mind. Ben said, "Go on with her. I can tend to the other business by myself. Mr. Anderson–Hub–you ain't commented. You needn't feel obligated, it's not your problem, after all."

Hub considered. This would put his plans aside for a while, but they needed his help and he couldn't leave in the middle of trouble. "No, I'm enlisted for the duration. Don't worry about me."

John had no idea how far they'd come, and little of direction. He knew they'd left the Llano river far behind, though, and climbed into higher elevations. The air was cooler. The ground was very rocky, carpeted with small, flat chunks of limestone. The oak and mesquite grew smaller; there was much prickly pear and the thorny scrub of the desert.

Something darker than the night was before them–the face of a tall cliff, and along this wall they led the horses in single file for perhaps two hundred yards and then were inside a bowl-shaped valley surrounded by dark risings. An oval shadow cast by starlight became the entrance to a cavern. It was from this place they'd made the long and dangerous journey searching for him.

Inside, a fire lit the interior. A passage led back into the mountain from the big room where the people had made themselves a hiding place. Sleeping robes were spread along one wall, a child, a small girl, asleep there. A woman was at the fire, bent over a cooking pot. He smelled food and remembered he had not eaten all day, but he felt no true hunger. The woman at the fire saw the wounded girl and came to her with soft, maternal sounds and took her into the passage away from the rest. John stood in a kind of sleepy trance as two men went outside to care for the horses.

Someone he hadn't seen before came into the light–a black man, smiling and holding out a hand to him. "Charlie Boone." It felt strange. John wasn't used to the offer of men's hands. "I know I'm a surprise to you, but I hear you the brand new chief of this here tribe."

He could only shake his head. Boone went on, "Well, either

46

way I can see you a tired boy tonight. Lay yourself down over there on Old Song's robe." He pointed. "Pore gal don't need it no more." The woman's body was near the entrance where they had left it, wrapped in the same buffalo robe they'd used on him. Boone said, "We can talk in the morning."

The experience had taken on the quality of a dream. Shadows and bursts of light from the fire circled the cave walls and ceiling. People moved slowly and their talk was low, the words carrying no more meaning to John than the sound of wind. A sudden memory of home, his mother, his bed. Loss and fear. He hated the idea of using the old woman's bed, but he, not much more than a child, had not the energy to argue.

Ben Turner led the mule through the stone-littered landscape, reins tight in his hand, the animal shying at every unexpected sound. Manning held himself in the saddle by gripping the horn, swaying in dangerous directions when the mule jumped. Neither spoke, but Ben knew his burden was conscious and awake. Ben had lashed the carbine in its scabbard so the man couldn't remove it if he decided to try. The pistol at his waist was weapon enough for now.

As he walked he held a silent conversation with himself. He resented having to do this. He ought to be with the others hunting for John, not nursing this big pile of hate.

But, looked at cooly, there'd been no choice. Left out here alone the man would surely die before they could return for him. The whispered accusation had to be a lie. John would never have shot him in cold blood. The truth would be something very different, but what would Dugan believe, sitting there behind his little desk and his little badge? Would he come after the boy? And what about all those tracks back there? Manning had said they were Indians and Ben had seen the moccasin prints himself, but who were they and why had they taken his grandson?

Better for the Turner family if Manning had died and his lies with him, but here was Ben doing the very thing that would save the very life that might doom the boy. The reins were almost yanked out of his hand when the mule jerked his head back. A rushing noise filled the brush, the dull impact of thorn on horn as large bodies tore through it, snorting anger and fear. He smelled the sudden odor of cattle, a herd of the wild ones bedded for the night and now disturbed and running. He was hours from home yet. He wondered if his legs would make it.

The splashing of swift-running water ahead caused him to wince in anticipation of crossing the stream he knew to be waist-high. It would leave him chilled and uncomfortable in the cooling night. He entered it holding his pistol and the reins above his head. The mule followed without protest and then stopped in the middle to drink. When the sorrel head bent down the dark presence in the saddle began to slip to the side.

A whispered "Help me!" And Manning fell into the current.

CHAPTER 9

Hub Anderson put himself into the lead, Sarah riding behind him followed closely by Harper. There was much less interference with them now, the trees had thinned out and almost disappeared except for the mesquites. Oaks grew small in the higher reaches of the uplift, twisted in a never-ending search for nutrients and water, but that struggle produced a beauty of its own, not appreciated by every eye. Hub thought the scene before him was perfect in the near light before dawn– a cleanness of earth and air he hadn't found in lower places. A starkness that suited him.

And somewhere nearby was the boy and the other people, whoever they might be. Hub, Sarah and James had ridden hard and moved swiftly. No one could have done more.

He looked behind at the woman. "We'll catch up pretty soon now. You want to rest a little?" She shook her head with a quick vigor. The dog had been silent for some time now. He might have stopped trailing to sleep, but Hub suspected he'd caught up to John's party and either they had killed him or the boy was free to quiet him down.

They were all weary. Whether Sarah liked it or not they'd soon have to unsaddle and allow the horses time to rest and graze the stingy grass.

To the north a mile or more a mesa blocked part of the gray

sky, and a softer mass fed down its slope, indicating trees that would have their feet in a source of water. He guided toward it. The first early blue appeared in the eastern sky, and clouds edged in hues of red. Some weather beginning to build up, maybe. His mouth was dry–tasted stained. Nearby a flock of buzzards left their roost with wide, powerful strokes, the sound of their wings loud in the still, cool morning. His stomach felt flat, craving food. The muscles across his shoulders and back burned with fatigue.

Hub knew he was in better shape physically than the other two, and knew they must be suffering more. He looked back at Sarah again. She stared ahead. Farther back, Harper shook his head in mild disapproval at her insistence. Hub didn't respond. They had no choice here, disapproval or not.

"Call in your hound," he said to Sarah. "He must be somewhere close."

Her attempt was scratchy, deep in her chest. She couldn't have been heard at much distance, but they waited for some minutes. She said, "He's too far."

"Reckon so." He tried a smile at her. Still, the dog's silence was a worry. If he'd caught up with the other riders then they were alerted to followers.

"Where are we?" She complained, her voice like dark smoke. "We're just wandering around, and Johnny could be anywhere."

Hub stopped the mare and pointed to the clear, deep track of a shod horse in the thin dirt. The woman took in a sharp breath of surprise. They rode abreast then, the country open enough to allow free movement, unlike the dense timber they'd battled through much of the night. At his left elbow James said, "You think they're up there at the foot of that mesa?"

"Maybe." He was glad James had noticed the same thing. Made him feel less alone. But he wasn't sure he thought that. In fact, he was far from sure about any of this. There was still a chance the boy had gone willingly. They were Indians, if Manning could be believed. Some were hurt, judging from the amount of blood back there in the rocks by the river. Could be John was hurt, though he had not dared mention it. In any event those up ahead were not likely to welcome riders on their trail and it was getting to be time for caution. Nothing but instinct was guiding him, but it was an instinct born of much experience.

A sharp metallic scratch brought him up straight in the saddle, reaching too late for his Winchester. Three horsemen charged into sight from an arroyo that cut the earth ahead like a scornful mouth. The mare reacted violently, tried to turn back, but he kept her planted. He recognized one of the riders. "It's John," he said. The boy rode the huge horse he'd taken from Manning. The others were Comanches, one carrying a bow, the other a carbine. It had been the sound of a cartridge levered into place in that weapon he'd heard. Hub was unhappy with himself. Too slow to react, not in fighting trim, and tired.

Sarah flashed off the pinto and rushed to stand beside her son's mount. John slid down and embraced her. "I think we can relax, James," Hub said. "Looks like everything's all right." The Indians lowered their weapons as Sarah talked to them, then mother and son came forward leading the big horse. The others kept their distance, but showed no menace.

"These people are from a small band of Comanches," she said, "remnants of the *Antelope Eaters*. This has all happened because of my crazy words in town." She brushed her son's arm, then raised her hands in a gesture of helplessness, bowing her head as though grieved or praying. James got down and stood beside her, his arm around her shoulders.

Hub dismounted, too, tired of riding, tired of the saddle, hurting. "Feels good to stand on my own feet." He looked at John. "We have come a long way, son. You've got a story to tell and I plan to hear it. You talk and we'll listen."

The sorrel mule finished drinking and waded out of the rushing creek onto the dry bank and stopped there in a nest of water-encouraged grass, tearing great mouthfuls from their roots despite the bit, unmindful of the steel impediment between his teeth. Water black as the night dripped from his belly and legs. Now and then he exhausted the supply of grass before him and he moved forward or to the side, causing the dangling stirrups to swing away from his body and back again. He paid no mind to the voice cursing somewhere in the distance, coming nearer now, and only raised his head at the last instant, beginning to move away when Benjamin's hand closed on the trailing reins and forced him to follow.

They walked a surprising distance because it had taken Ben a long time to catch up to the large body being carried away in the current and in the end he had struggled with the last of his strength and his one arm to haul the oversized man out by holding to a wet boot and pulling until he saw a glint of starlight on Manning's face as it flopped onto the sloping creekbank.

The dark mound ahead moved feebly, striving for breath. The mule shied back and got enough slack in the reins to drop his head and snatch another mouthful of grass.

"Get up, Manning. I can't put you in the saddle."

"Tried to drown me." Barely a whisper.

"I may yet do it if you don't climb on this beast. I want to get home."

The remounting presented its difficulties, but when it was done they resumed the trail, and as he walked Ben wondered at his own actions tonight. When Manning went into the water it was simple and good counsel to just let him drown. The body would wash up somewhere and his compadres would find him with lungs full of water and a bullet somewhere in that bull of a chest. No matter what they found there'd be nobody to point a finger at John Turner.

But even while these thoughts went through his mind he had found himself leaping into the current, fighting his way over the rocks and tangled branches, intent on rescue. Now what?

Get home first, give the man whatever help he could with the wound, and that would be considerable because Ben had spent

52

a lifetime on the frontier and couldn't begin to count the bullets he'd gouged out of hurt men, the wounds he'd treated–sometimes his own. But what then? He looked up into the stars that had begun to fade. No answer there and a new morning coming.

The Comanches had filled the neck of a narrow canyon with stones, creating a corral for their horses shaded by a stratum of limestone tilted at an odd angle. Hub unsaddled his mare and helped the others, and they turned the mounts loose inside. The spring of water that gave rise to the patch of greenery he'd first noted from across the wide valley had been partially diverted to a natural rock hollow inside the corral. There the horses and the people drank. Hub felt as hollow as the rock, his strong body worn down by the night of riding. He was hungry, but it was sleep that made the strongest demand. He could see that James and Sarah were almost out on their feet. The hound that had led them here was tied by a length of rope, asleep in the shade.

The cave's interior was a cool surprise. Probably ancestors of these very people, or people like them, had lived here long ago. It had everything a small group of primitive people would need–water, game in the surrounding countryside, safety from weather and from enemies. Was it possible man had once needed only that? Other figures moved around inside. Something was wrapped in a buffalo robe near the entrance. He was too tired to pay attention.

John seemed anxious to talk, but his mother said to him, "There's much to talk about, son, but let us sleep just a little and then we'll talk." The woman from the cook pot motioned them down the passage to a rocky ell, the space she and her family occupied according to Sarah's translation. Blankets and robes lay on the floor. The men removed their gunbelts and shucked their boots. Hub was careful to put himself close against the wall, leaving room for James to lie next to the blonde woman. Sarah stood for a few moments after the men were prone on the floor, her look of uncertainty plain even in the semi-darkness, then she lay down an arm's length from Harper and despite the voices close by, the noise and the odors of food and smoke and the gamey stink of the buffalo robes, all three were asleep in less than a minute.

CHAPTER 10

Captain Emil Dugan took his time over breakfast. It was his favorite meal of the day, and the small man ate a good deal more food of a morning than men twice his size. Part of his appetite came from his late-night sessions of love making in the room upstairs, but mostly it was a puzzle to him how he could eat so well, yet remain slender and muscular, never gaining the fat he saw accumulate on others.

It was a secret point of pride, but not the only one.

He also liked the sound of his voice and his ability to use language in a way that made other men pay attention. And he was proud of the beautiful woman still asleep. Proud, that is, of himself, that he could attract and keep such a woman. And the money. Oh, yes, very proud of the money indeed. The very source of his power. It had been some time now since he had opened the safe and counted it, perhaps something he should do today.

Two early drinkers stood at the bar sipping beers, otherwise he was the only patron. The saloon didn't like to serve breakfast, but he had insisted and now they managed it very well. He flicked a piece of stray bacon off the front of his starched white shirt and put another bite of fried egg in his mouth, chewing slowly, followed the egg with a mouthful of buttered biscuit sopped in honey and washed it all down with a long swallow of coffee. He explored the tastes of the food, ignoring the figure standing beside his chair, the trooper called Cooter, who rightly feared interrupting his meal. Dugan noted that the barman and the drinkers grew uneasy while the silent Cooter waited his cue to speak

And that was part of his power as well–his ability to cause fear while simply having breakfast. He felt great satisfaction with his life.

He put down his fork and said, "What is it?" The fellow had the kind of country-simple face seen so often on the frontier– born to serve others, not an original thought in the misshapen head. Dugan noted that a yellowish matter had dried in the corners of Cooter's eyes overnight.

"Captain, that patrol that went out yestiddy?"

"What about it?" He remembered the patrol well, since he'd assigned it to three men he wanted to punish, and a long ride through the hot countryside seemed a good enough method.

"They never come back in, sir." That was odd. If he had thought about it at all he would have expected them back by nightfall. Maybe they'd run into a band of outlaws, always a possibility. Dugan considered the news.

"All right. Go back to the office. I'll be along soon." He filled his fork with another bite of eggs and waited until the man reached the door, then called out in a loud voice that everyone in the room could hear.

"And Cooter?"

"Yes, sir?"

"Wash your face."

Hub woke up wanting hot coffee and a few more hours of sleep, but the possibility of either was remote. James was still unconscious beside him, snoring softly. Sarah was gone. He cranked himself up, hurting in the back and legs, emitting a groan that was almost a laugh. He got on his boots and gunbelt, and with the familiar weight tugging at his hips nudged James in the ribs and extended an arm to help him off the floor.

"Goshallmighty," James whispered, "I feel like I been beat to death."

"You'll feel better when you move around some." Hub left him to finish dressing and walked into the main room. The sun was well up and the cave had taken on some of the heat from outside. He felt sweat trickle down his spine beneath his shirt, and smelled the stink that had dried into his garments.

An old Comanche man wearing a breechclout, the thigh of his right leg wrapped in a bandage, stood in the entrance just out of the sun's reach, peering into the valley. Curious, Hub walked over and took a look himself, saw nothing but heat waves rising.

"He's just keeping watch." Sarah was on her knees beside what looked to be a pile of robes. Her long dress had become a shapeless mass that blurred her figure and hid her legs and ankles. She had combed her hair and appeared more rested, but her sadness was evident.

"What's wrong?"

"This. The woman they killed. Her name was *Old Song*. She was the first wife of Two Hawks. We lived together many years." A single tear worked down her cheek.

"Well I'm sorry to hear it. Bad luck all the way around. Where's your boy?"

"Gone for a walk outside." James Harper appeared, tugging at his trousers with one hand, trying to smooth down his hair with the other.

"Sarah? What's the matter?" She shook her head, bit down on her lower lip and didn't reply.

Hub told him, "She's grieved over this woman here that they killed." James nodded in partial understanding.

Sarah patted the mound as though to comfort her old friend, sighed and rose from the floor in one graceful motion. "You men should eat now. There's plenty of food. And there's someone here you'll want to meet." She led them farther inside the cavern. Kerosene lamps lit the way. Was it coffee they smelled?

57

The man was the color of twilight, not quite black–a blend of grays and browns with teeth that shone white in a pleasant face. He was roosted on a stool against the far wall. "Hope you can spare some of that coffee," James said. The man lifted his cup in a mock salute.

"Got your cups cooling, gentlemen. Right over here." He motioned to a spread blanket containing food in what looked like military mess kits. "Everybody around this place but me sit on the floor, but I got to have a little furniture."

Sarah said, "This is Charlie Boone. James Harper and Hubbard Anderson." The two nodded, almost too hungry for even that small gesture, before putting themselves crosslegged on the blanket and starting on the meat and bread. It was venison, stewed rather than fried like the steaks they had abandoned when the boy went missing. A blackened kettle simmered over a small fire that sent a tiny rill of smoke up to a hole in the roof, and from the hole a bit of sunshine edged its way inside.

After a few bites of the meat Harper swallowed some coffee from his tin cup and said, "This is quite a surprise Mr. Boone. The venison, the coffee for sure, and you in particular." He glanced at Sarah. "I suspect there's a good story here."

"I do say so myself, I believe you right," Boone said, drawing some coffee from his own cup. "Don't call me no *mistah* though. You can call me Charlie, or *Black Charlie* if you want to, won't offend me none. I knowed the name *Black Charlie* my whole life and it sound like rain on the roof to me." His words seemed to carry a hint of challenge, but the effect was smoothed by his good humor.

The food had an immediate effect on Hub. He felt his accustomed strength returning. There were plenty of questions he wanted answers to, but it was James who said, "The obvious question is pretty simple. Who are you and what are you doing here?" James filled his mouth with bread and meat and waited. Boone sipped at the cup in his hand and enough time went by that it appeared he wasn't going to reply. Then he blinked his eyes as if coming back from distant thoughts and smiled at them.

He stood up from the stool, spilling a bit of his coffee as he did it and said, "Sit here, ma'am. Believe I'll tell it standing up." Sarah protested, but he continued motioning to her and finally she sat down.

"Got a touch of arthuritis," he said. He lodged a hand in the small of his back and stretched. "Need to stand up a while. Yes, sir, that's better all right. Well, who I am is Charlie Boone, like the lady say. Emancipated slave of the late Colonel Buford Boone of South Carolina. The colonel was shot dead some place the name of which I never heard. When the yankee soldiers come tell us we was free I left with the clothes on my back and his name, because I didn't have one of my own and he didn't need it no more."

There was bitterness in the words and maybe more, but Hub felt no offense. In his view a man once owned by other men had some right to bitterness.

To James Boone said, "What was that other question?"

"Just...what you're doing out here. What *all* these people are doing out here."

"Well, a course what they are doing is hiding. Else white man kill 'em or put 'em up at Fort Sill with the rest of their folks."

"You hiding, too?" Hub regretted saying it because Sarah shot him a quick, dark look. "No offense meant."

Boone finished his coffee, put the cup down and said, "I guess so. Went wandering a while when we was freed. Wanted to see the countryside. And I seen it. Seen I supposed to keep on being *Black Charlie* though I free now. I come across these ragged folks and they let me stay. Had myself a little money and I give it to 'em and they use it for necessaries. Put on Mexican clothes and go off to buy food and things with it. Ain't no buffalo out here you know. Some wild cattle, deer, fish in the rivers. They know Spanish. I teach 'em a little English." He pointed to James' cup. "You sold us that coffee you're drinking right now, at your store over in Kimbleville."

James thought it over. "Two vaqueros? Paid for it with silver? I remember. Not many people come in carrying silver."

There was silence in the room then, broken only by the noise of forks on the tin plates as they finished eating. Boone lifted a decorated skin pouch from the floor and got out a pipe, filled it with tobacco and lit it. He laughed. "The Indians, they can't figure me smoking this pipe just for pleasure. Only time *they* do it everything all solemn, you know, blow it thisaway, thataway, up and down and pass it all around. Y'all want some more meat? Plenty coffee."

Sarah took the pot from the edge of the fire and filled their cups.

"What about us?" Hub gestured at James and himself. "Aren't you taking a chance telling us these things?"

"Why, you different sorts, ain't you? This lady is mama to the new chief, and she already told me you her friends. That's how come my mouth been at a fast trot."

Boone seemed straightforward enough, though there were some gaps in his story. But for Hub, like most of the things that had happened lately, it wasn't his business anyway. Better to keep quiet and let the others work things out as they wished. He could get about the things he'd come for.

But where did an ex-slave get silver? Had he stolen it? Killed for it? He didn't mourn the death of his master, but that was natural enough. A good story there, probably, but one Hub wasn't going to hear. Any rate, the boy was safe. James was a lucky man if the blonde woman was really his for the rest of his life, but Hub couldn't help wondering about that, too. James acted like the marriage was all but done while she appeared less certain. Anybody could see fondness and friendship between them, but love?

James interrupted his thoughts.

"We need to head for home. That store of mine won't run itself any longer."

Boone took note of his words. "Won't be no gossipin' about what you seen here, I reckon?" Hub silently shook his head.

60

James went on, "Nobody will hear anything from us."Sarah picked up the conversation. "I have yet to talk to John. He's avoiding me and I'm afraid of what that means. Point of fact, I think he plans to stay and not come back home with us." "I don't want to intrude in your business," James said, "But it might be best if he does. If Manning lives to tell his claims that John's responsible for what happened to him, you know what Dugan will do."

"Do you think that will make any difference?"

"I guess you're right." To Boone she said, "Will there be a ceremony for *Old Song*?"

"Pretty soon, I reckon. Everybody waiting on me."

"What do you mean?"

"I their holy man, you see. I can tell it surprise you, but if you think about it, it ain't much of a mystery. They used to red skin and more white skin than they want to see, but *black* skin? No, sir. It's the skin they think is holy. I just the man inside it. And acourse they think it all magic the way you hand over some paper money or coins to a store clerk and he hand you back a rifle or a sack of flour.

"Normal thing for them is if somebody got something you want you trade him for it, or you just kill him and take it. I am what you call a brand new concept all the way around. Also I am the tribe undertaker. So y'all scuse me and I'll dress up for it and be out yonder in a minute."

Sarah gathered the dirty dishes, both men offering to help and each getting a clipped refusal. She followed them to the cavern entrance, handed James a hunk of greasy meat and said, "When you check on the horses, give this to the dog, will you? He's in the corral if he didn't follow Johnny off. And fill this bucket with water."

They put on their hats and went out in the midday sun. The hound was nowhere to be seen. Hub said, "Put it over by the water. He'll find it when he comes in. Probably caught a rabbit by now, anyway."

61

Their horses looked rested. There was a trough filled with corn, and even a block of salt. Hub lifted the hoofs of his mare and found her feet clean and healthy. He let James struggle alone with his Appaloosa. Offering help might be seen as an insult. It was anybody's guess what horse Sarah would be riding home, but the pinto was all right.

Lugging the heavy water bucket back into the mouth of the cave they ran into the Comanches who were coming outside. Some bent their bodies with ritual cries of grief. Charlie Boone appeared, naked but for a loincloth and moccasins and a scrap of beaded leather over his bald head, hiding all of his face except his eyes. Behind him was Sarah.

James groaned when he saw her. She had cut her long hair, and blood ran down her face from knife wounds across her cheeks and forehead. She walked defiantly past the two men as if they were not there.

CHAPTER 11

The walk had been an excuse to spend time with the Comanche girl. Since they'd arrived he'd had no chance to talk to her, learn more about her, but she aroused very strong feelings in him–feelings so powerful he could think of little else. And now that they were safer, now that Sarah was released from anxiety about him, he searched through the cavern and found her resting against a wall, wrapped in a soft blue blanket. Her eyes were shut and he thought at first she was asleep.

He felt himself respond to the beauty of her face, the memory of lithe movement as she climbed or leaped or simply walked, the way she had stared into his eyes when she gave him the knife out of her own bosom.

True, he'd known no other girls well, but it didn't matter. There was no girl like this one, and though he didn't even know her name there was already an unspoken bond between them. Surely she could feel it, too. She knew enough of his language to teach him hers–the language Sarah had refused to speak or teach despite his requests growing up. This beautiful girl could teach him what he wanted to learn; not just language, but customs, the ways of the people. *His* people.

Her father, mother and sister sat nearby, eating and talking among themselves and watching his discomfort. Should he go over and wake her? Call to her? Ask permission? And just how

63

would he do that, not knowing the language?

The child solved the problem for him. She rose, took three steps with a tiny fist balled up and banged her sister on the head, nodding with satisfaction as the closed eyes opened and the girl reached out in good-natured menace at the retreating little one. She saw John.

She said, "Not sleep."

"Everybody's tired, I know. I was wondering...I thought I'd go for a walk outside, try to get a handle on things."

"Handle?"

"I just mean, think about everything, you know? And maybe you can tell me stuff. Can you come with me for a while?"

"Walk out this cave?"

"Yeah. Not far, though."

She said something to her parents and stood up, unwrapping the blanket from herself and folding it. "Old day not good I come with you. Now is different. I show you talk?"

"Yeah, that's what I want. You show me Comanche talk." He couldn't take his eyes off the dimple centered in her left cheek. Were the parents allowing her to go with him, or had she simply decided on her own? He glanced at the stoic faces and inclined his head to them, feeling foolish.

As they prepared to leave, the father got to his feet and began to gesture and speak to the girl, who listened with respect, nodding in agreement. John realized he was taller than the adult man, this man who'd carried him helpless through the woods, kidnapped him from his own barnyard. He had seemed so fearsome then; now he was just a short Indian with bowed legs from a lifetime on horseback, animated and agile as a jackrabbit. Finished talking, he looked from his daughter to John and waited for her to translate his words.

"Father say...careful. Go short time, not far time. No man see. You do head now, we go."

"Do head? Oh, you mean this." He nodded to the man and got a softer look from the black eyes in return. He followed her out, heard her laughter, wondered what she found funny.

Sarah sat beside the old woman's body. She wanted him to stay with her, but let him leave without hindrance when she recognized the boy's intent to be alone with the Comanche girl. Everything, it seemed, was changing with such speed and power she couldn't stop it. Now this sense of loss. This child of hers looking elsewhere. She watched him touch the girl's arm, noted the muscles of his shoulders. They must have been there all along. Why had she not noticed before that he was becoming a man?

John untied the hound and let him come along. They went through the corral and followed the canyon to a trail she showed him. It led them down the mountain to a hidden world John could hardly believe. Up above was sun and thorn, rock and dust and sweat. Here, rounded boulders nested like enormous eggs in tall grass, spring water raised cooling vapors into the air, and liquid fingers felt their way between the trunks of cottonwood and cypress trees.

There was constant movement in the trees, birds, squirrels playing chase, leaping great distances between branches. A large crane lifted itself from the grass on ponderous wings when the dog barked, and with a grating call flew away.

"Beautiful," he said.

"Oh, yes, I know that word."

"So are you."

"*Sar?*" She didn't understand him.

"So..are...you. Beautiful." A slight blush crept into her tawny skin, and her eyes sought the ground. She turned away, hiding her face, and with a skipping motion found a spring of water with a handy boulder and leaned over the stone to drink.

He watched her movements, full of the sense that something new had come into his life and that nothing he'd known would be the same again. The realization carried small tremors of sadness, but an almost overpowering feeling of elation and adventure. He took a seat beside her.

"Tell me your name."

She hesitated, then said, "Say *Arbole Alta.*"

"That's Spanish. I meant what I speak. English."

"English say *Tall Tree*. Name of me."

"Well, you have a pretty name. I like the Spanish best. I'll call you Alta. Alta..." He said it again because he liked saying it, round and lovely on his tongue. "I say you Alta. Okay?"

"Alta me? John you?" His name did not leave her mouth easily, the unaccustomed hard consonant lost.

Their communication was slow, each striving to understand the other. What dangers did they face? What was the best answer to their plight, and what was his role to be? He was certain of one thing–they were his people and he would never abandon them to fate.

After an hour she stood and said, "Go now. Abuela."

"The old woman?"

"Yes." She took his hand.

Sarah watched the young couple arrive, jealous still that the boy had chosen someone else instead of coming to her with his uncertainties. Still, he was alive and well, and after the fears she'd carried during the night-long ride, their present situation was almost welcome.

She listened to the wails of mourning from the people–pitifully few at that, but only a few tears came from her own eyes. Yes, it hurt that Old Song was dead, but she had long since mourned the loss of this woman, her husband, the tribe itself, mourned them and put them away. In her mind Old Song had died long ago.

The black man shuffled his feet slowly in the dust, shook a gourd rattle. The corpse was dressed in her best clothing and wrapped in a blanket and laid on a travois. This was not to be a burial such as those Sarah had witnessed many times, the body placed high on a platform in a sacred place, lifted up from the earth and seen easily from a distance. No, this was to be expedient and necessary, and Boone had convinced them that those factors made it also right.

Soon the woman would be taken far from the camp and left alone on a nameless mesa so that wild birds and animals might consume her flesh, leaving no evidence of who she had been, or the meaning of scattered bones in a far, far place.

There would be scars on Sarah's face from the knife wounds she had inflicted today. The beauty that had so captivated James Harper would be marred. She wondered if it would make a difference in his feelings for her, wondered if he would now think her barbaric, force him to consider her with new thoughts and imaginings.

Was he ashamed before the eyes of his friend? Hub Anderson was a good friend, to be sure. Only a little thoughtless in his remarks sometimes as any man might be. There was something a little frightening about him. Something that might overpower his decency if he was pushed too hard. It had been in his face on the street in town, a fierceness that might have taken him in any direction, over any obstacle.

And she knew why it had seemed so familiar. It was the look she had often seen on the face of Two Hawks when anger had pushed him beyond control–when death was on the wind.

Her gaze wandered, found James and Hub in the shade of the cavern. Neither could have guessed–not even her son or father could have guessed–how much of those wild times were hidden away inside her. How much barbarity, even ruthlessness, she owned and could call upon if necessary.

CHAPTER 12

Ben Turner removed his soiled clothing, weak and needing
the support of the bed as he half-stood half-lay at the edge and
greadually let himself fall across the spread, relief so powerful
tears came to his eyes for a moment.

What a night. The injured man slept in the bunkhouse after
more than an hour of agonizing probing for the bullet in his
chest, Ben slow and careful to do as little injury as possible to
heart and lung. And miraculously, when he thought he'd have
to give up and leave it, there it was at the surface, bloody, flat
from the impact, half-hidden by torn tissue. It fell to the floor
with a heavy, hollow sound. Mindless lead weight, flinging
itself here and there, into and out of things or people or skies,
taking life, saving life, who knew?

Manning had cursed him while he labored until enough
whiskey had gone down to silence him. Too much whiskey,
maybe, in his weakened condition. Enough to kill him? Ben
had not cared. The ironic truth was that while he worked to
save the wounded man he would have been happier had the
patient died. Tonight everything was two-faced.

He'd continued far past the limits of his own endurance and
was physically and emotionally empty when he'd wrapped the
huge chest in a torn white sheet and left the small building.

Worn out as he was, Ben found the strength to fumble together corn and water for the mule, who shoved his nose into the trough without regard for the hand that stroked his neck as he ate.

Had he ever been so tired? Sleep was slow coming, advancing on him, then retreating as he thought of the others still somewhere in the hills, John alive? Dead? He had to sleep. Had to. And yet it meant letting go for a time and so he kept his attention focused as if remaining awake he might alter threat with the force of his own desires.

He was unaware when his thoughts became fanciful and capered off in unbidden directions and, no longer awake, he was lifted out of his fears and made at peace, if only for a little while.

Charlie Boone had left with the old woman's body for a secret place and the other people had gathered inside the cavern. Sarah took James' arm and motioned to Hub and John and the four went outside again. Harper's horse was already saddled.

She said, "Are you planning to go back alone?"

"Wouldn't say planning, but I'm going real soon. I'll wait for anybody else wants to come along." Hub could hear the frustration in his friend's voice.

To her son she said, "What are you going to do, John? You owe me at least an explanation."

He shook his head silently. He would not leave Alta, but staying here was dangerous. It was a bad situation and he didn't know the answer. Sarah seemed to understand his confusion.

"Do you think they would come to the ranch?" The thought would have been an impossibility even a week earlier, but Ben Turner had changed. "Maybe we could hide them there, keep you safe."

James spoke up. "That's crazy, Sarah. Anyway, Ben won't allow it."

69

She stared at him until he lowered his eyes. The day was already hot and all around them the dry countryside shimmered in a great, sweeping silence. He walked over to his Appaloosa, tightened the cinch, checked over his rigging.

"Would grandpa let them stay?"

"I think so, yes. I'll go back with James and talk to him." She called out, "Wait, James, I'm going with you." To John she said, "You stay here until I get word back to you."

Harper glanced at Hub. "You coming?"

"I'll be along, but I think I'll scout out the country some since I'm out here. See if I can find some cows. Tell Ben I'll be there in a day or two and ready to work."

That was the truth, but not his only reason to let James and Sarah ride alone. There had been a change of some sort in the woman. She'd taken on a hint of wildness he hadn't seen before. James sensed it, too, plus he was jealous and Hub couldn't figure out why. Had he said or done anything to cause it? She was a beauty, no denying it, but his mind was on catching cattle, not stealing his friend's girl. Those two needed time alone to talk.

Sarah looked at him as if he'd surprised her, and then there was something else in the blue eyes. She'd read his thoughts, but he could not read hers.

The loosed hound fell into step with the two horses as they prepared to leave. Harper said, "When will you be back in town? We never got the chance to talk over old times as much as I wanted."

Hub shrugged. "Guess that'll depend on how much cooperation I get from the cows, James. But I won't leave for home without a visit." He was glad to see that his friend's spirits had lifted, and he knew the reason of course–James would be alone on the trail with Sarah for a day and much of a night. And despite her ravaged hair and wounded face, such a beauty would be a welcome companion for any man on any journey.

Emil Dugan walked his horse at the head of the short column–his sergeant and three men they'd recruited from the saloon crowd, men whose pay came out of his own treasury. Men who would do anything he told them to do. The two he'd sent ahead earlier had not returned. Perhaps they'd found sign of the missing men. It might do to haul in for a while and wait, but waiting had never been a part of Dugan's methods. Forward, always forward, was his way as the men of his Ohio company had learned in the late war. Very few of those men were left to curse his memory.

He lit a cigar, scratching the match across the pommel of his saddle, tapping a heel into the horse's flank and picking up the pace to a slow trot. Behind him the others did the same.

They had been riding much of the day. Something had happened to three of his men and he meant to find out what. No matter that they were difficult men with discipline problems, drinking problems. They were his responsibility. They should have returned with a full report long before now.

Far ahead to the west he heard three gunshots close together, the signal he'd been listening for, and spurred his mount into a lope, the cigar pinned between his teeth, its lit end red as a probing eye.

The sound of the shots had traveled farther that he'd thought and it took many minutes of purposeful riding for them to arrive. He looked back with disgust at the straggle of men and horses coming up to join him. He would save chastisement for another time, it would serve no purpose now. He dismounted and handed the reins to a man standing there.

"What have you found?"

"A grave, sir. Signs of a fight."

"One dead?"

"Two. Reeves and Gonzales, in the same hole."

"There was a third man with them. Any sign of him?"

"Manning? No, sir."

"What about their horses?"

"Ain't found any yet, captain."

"Tracks?"

"There's a bunch goes off north, and we found the track of a single animal and the boot prints of a man–looks to me like he was leading it, headed east of here."

Dugan thought it over in silence, puffing on the cigar, working a pattern into the dust with the toe of his boot. "Rebury the two men, then. Dig a second grave and be sure to cover both with adequate rocks. This is as good a resting place as any, I suppose. Fashion two markers for the graves, as well. I'll say a few words over them as soon as you're finished."

All his troop had dismounted and the men had spread into the surrounding area on foot. One of them called out to him.

There was blood on a boulder, and also in a small aperture where two of the granite uplifts converged. And in the sandy soil were footprints, not the hard edges of bootheels, but smooth indentations.

"Them's moc'sins, Captain," one of his men said. "This here musta been a indin fight."

When he had completed the formalities of burial Dugan called his men together and said to his sergeant, "Billings, I want you to take three men and follow this trail north, see what you find. My guess is it's a renegade band off the reservation."

"How far do you want me to follow them, Captain?"

"No more than a day's ride, I think. It's likely they left this country after the fight, but prudence dictates we make sure. The rest of us will pitch in our rations. You'll be all right for a couple of days."

"What about that set of tracks heading east?"

Dugan smiled and got another cigar out of his pocket. "I believe I have that figured out, Sergeant. In part, at least. Forget about it." He knelt to scratch a match on one of the granite knobs and lit the cigar.

"We'll return to town tonight. I'll expect to hear your report in two days. Understood?"

Billings and the three riders continued north until it became too dark to see and made camp under the limbs of a live oak.

They were tired. The hobbled horses grazed close by. The men talked little, ate a spare supper and slept early. Their small fire burned slowly down to ashes.

CHAPTER 13

It was that fire James saw as he and Sarah rode in silence into the night. They were weary and not in good temper, and the ride had been nothing like what he'd hoped for. There had been no intimacy, no sharing of dreams, no plans for a future. Her concern was for her son, for the Comanche people. In her thoughts his desires did not exist. Maybe *he* didn't exist. James understood that his feelings were a little childish, selfish even, but he had been patient for a very long time.

Still, this was neither the time or place to assert himself, make demands. He would wait longer yet. As he'd told Hub, Sarah was worth it. He halted the Appaloosa.

"Campfire ahead."

"Who could it be?"

"No idea. Don't reckon it's anybody we want to visit with, though. Stay close and keep that hound with us, too." They circled the camp, forcing the horses through a dense cedar brake that gave James a good deal of trouble. "Times like this," he muttered at one point, "is when I wish I'd let 'em whack the doggone leg off."

The moon had risen when they reached the Turner ranch. Sarah was relieved that James rode on after a few minutes of conversation with Ben. He expected too much from her right now and she could think of nothing but her son's danger.

Tired as she was she resolved to check on the wounded Manning before sleeping, see for herself his condition. She wished they'd left him to die–wished it a thousand times over. It was what he deserved.

He was awake. His eyes shone in the lamplight. She felt the heat in his forehead. "Fever," she said. He looked up into her face without comment, an emptiness behind his eyes. Possibly he wouldn't make it anyway, save everybody trouble. She unwrapped the bandage. Ben had done a good job, but probing for the bullet had left the wound irritated and now it was infected, streaks of red in the surrounding tissue. Could turn to blood poisoning.

"Don't move. I'll be back." There was no response. Perhaps he didn't even hear her.

In the corner of her dark garden where herbs grew she pulled leaves from some of the plants, a tall blonde woman with her hair cut ragged, blood caked on her cheeks from the self-inflicted cuts of mourning. She had horrified her father, knew she would and hadn't cared. This was what a woman of her people did when a loved one died. The fault wasn't Ben's, nor was it hers. It was the fault of life, that's all, and through that fault she was as much a part of those native people as she was the white world. She would shrink from the knowledge no longer and Ben and everyone else would just have to let it be.

The herbs went into boiling water and were reduced to a steaming mass of pulp that she scooped into a cloth. She twisted the ends of the cloth and wrung out as much water as she could and then carried it out to the bunkhouse.

Manning lay in the same position, still unresponsive. From the look in his eyes there was a good chance he wouldn't live through another night. She hoped he would not in spite of what she was doing for him now.

She spread the warm poultice on the wound and bound him up again and left him there.

Ben tried to ignore the blood on her face. She said, "We may find him dead come morning."

"If he lives I'll haul him into town soon as the sun comes up."

"I think the ride in would finish him for sure."

"Well, then maybe I ought to go in alone and tell Dugan about him."

That frightened her. "What would you tell him?"

"Just...I don't know. We found him. Shot. Brought him here."

"You heard him, papa. He blames Johnny. They'll hunt him down. I can't let that happen."

"No. We can't." He poured a cup of coffee, stared through the window at the night outside. "Give it til morning. We'll see how he is then."

Tired as she was, Sarah could not sleep. She dozed a few hours, dreams running through her head like frightened deer, then woke in the small hours after midnight, a candle burning in the room, almost glad to be awake again, glad the dreams were only smoke. She lay still, remembering Ben's words. There was only one way to be sure Johnny was not blamed.

It would be hard, but she could do it, and she could live with the knowledge of it. She dressed again and used the candle to light her way out of the house. At the back door the old hound raised himself up to greet her and followed along the way to the bunkhouse. There was no wind, the night hot and close and filled with the sounds of insects like accusing voices. Stars shone like the bold and staring eyes of witnesses. Her heart beat fast, the pulse of her blood tingling in the tips of her fingers, fluttering at her throat. And yet she would do it.

In the moving shadows cast by candlelight lay Manning's inert form, his breathing loud and uncertain. From one of the bunks she took a pillow of strong ticking filled with feathers. The hand that held the flame shook. She needed both her hands and all her strength to do this and so found a table and pulled it close to the bunk and set the candle on it. She held the pillow in a desperate grip and leaned over him, gathered herself for the final act.

His eyes opened.

They stared at each other, hatred, fear, resignation and acceptance mingling in their gazes until Sarah could not have said which belonged to the man and which to her. His lips parted as if he wished to speak, but he made no sound. His eyes closed again. She sighed, waited for the return of resolution, the clear acceptance of her duty tipping on some internal scale.

She put the pillow back, took her candle and left the room. The hound followed her to the back door. In her own bedroom she snuffed the light and lay down to wait for dawn, listening to the simple, insistent beating of her own heart.

CHAPTER 14

A late breakfast was on the table when Ben returned. "Still alive," he said, hanging his hat by the door. "Fever's gone down. I reckon that poultice you made last night done some good. For *him,* anyway." There were eggs on their plates, and biscuits, but neither seemed inclined to eat. They sipped coffee silently until Sarah put her cup down hard.

"I have something to ask you." He looked up, waiting.

"There are six Comanche people living in the cave I told you about. And another one, an ex-slave. And now Johnny. One of them's a girl, probably sixteen or seventeen years old, and Johnny is...sweet on her. He's not going to just come back home and leave her out there. I know it."

Ben gave her a wistful smile. "Well, Sarah, it happens to every little boy sooner or later."

"You don't have to say it that way. I know he's not a little boy any longer. I accept that, even though it seems to've happened overnight. But what I'm saying is that he–and they– are in terrible danger. He could even be killed out there."

Ben said, "It will get worse when our patient talks to his boss."

"I want to bring them here." It took all her breath to get it out and then she could hardly breathe from the fear of what he'd say.

"You mean the whole bunch?"

"There's room. We have the barn, the bunkhouse. Nobody would know they're here."

"Oh, Sarah, I don't want that. All them people under out feet, have to watch out for 'em all the time. And feed 'em. It'll cost just to keep 'em fed. Not to mention Dugan and his bunch liable to come in here and tear the place apart."

"There are laws..."

"Yes, there are, and one of them is that the Indians is supposed to be up at Fort Sill with the rest of their likes. If we keep 'em here it's us breaking the law."

"But Dugan can't just come in here and..."

"No, course he can't. But he's liable to anyway." The hound began barking. Ben got up from the table and looked out a window.

"Our talk has conjured up the devil, Sarah. That's Dugan his self out there and a few of his men." He came back and took a last drink of coffee and stood there looking at her. "I think you ought to stay out of sight while they're around."

She opened her mouth to protest, but he interrupted. "Dugan's not dumb, Sarah. He sees you like that, he'll make something of it."

Her hand went to her face, felt the ridge of scab beginning there. He was right. Even though it galled her she would hide herself behind a shut door and leave it to her father to deal with them. The situation took on an unreal quality. Had she really tried to heal a man and also kill him on the same night?

"Very well, tell him I'm sick if he asks. I'll stay in my bedroom."

Ben came over to her and put his arms around her and kissed her cheek, and then without another word he went outside.

Dugan dismounted while the other two riders stayed in their saddles. "Good day, sir," the little dandy said. The man was a wonder. Their horses were sweated, the men's faces dusty from

79

travel, and here was Dugan with his string tie in place, his dress coat buttoned nice and not a stain on him.

"Water trough over there," Ben pointed at the corral. One of the riders took Dugan's reins and led the captain's horse behind his own mount. The men took off their hats in the shade while the horses plunged their faces into the water.

"Much obliged for the water," Dugan said. "The point of our visit is this–two of my men were killed yesterday in what looked like an Indian fight a few miles to the west. There was a third man with them. I think he may be alive. And I think you brought him here."

He was watching Ben carefully. Whatever the man's expectations, Ben didn't hesitate. He indicated the bunkhouse with a twist of his head. "Right over there."

Dugan appeared confused by the answer. Probably expecting a lie. "So I'm right? He is alive?"

"Yes, he is. But not lively. I wanted to haul him into town today in my wagon but I was afraid the trip might do him in."

When they entered the low room Manning's eyes were open. "How do you feel?" Dugan said. Manning tried to speak, but what came out was just a whisper of sound.

Ben said, "Bullet hit him in the chest. Clipped a lung, I think."

Dugan indicated the bandage. "It looks as if you've cared for him very well. Remarkable, if I may say so, after the incident on the street."

"I got the bullet out. My daughter put the poultice on him."

Dugan lifted his eyebrows and said with a hint of a smile, "Even more remarkable." Ben didn't trust the show of friendliness. This fellow was no friend to anyone but himself. Outside, Dugan called to the others to rest in the shade until he finished his business.

Then, to Ben he said, "Did you kill those men?"

"No, I did not." This was more like it–no pretense. Easier to handle. Also more frightening. The Captain had power, and he liked using it.

"By chance do you know who did?"

Ben shook his head. "Can't tell you much. That's how we found 'em." Too late realizing his mistake.

"We? Who else was with you?"

He worked at keeping his face open and honest. "The Anderson man. You remember him. Interested in buying some of my cattle. We heard the gun battle a long ways off, rode out there and by the time we found it everything was over, nobody there except your three on the ground, two dead and this one bad wounded."

"And where is Anderson now?"

Those eyes were intelligent, sharp. Ben said, "He didn't come back with me. Wanted to scout cattle some more."

"And your grandson? Where is he today?"

"Why, I can't answer that for sure. He went off by his self hunting this morning. He does that a lot. Be back by tonight, I expect."

"His horse is in your pasture."

"Oh, well, the pinto you mean. He don't hunt on horseback. Goes on foot."

"The stealthy savage?"

"Something like that, I reckon." Ben wanted to hit the smug face, but held the desire back, watched into the distance.

"Very well. I think you're telling me at least a near approximation of the truth. The killers would seem to be Indians. Have you seen any in this vicinity?"

"No, sir, I haven't. They're all on the reservation, far as I know." He'd just been called a liar, but too much hung in the balance. He couldn't react as he normally would and Dugan knew it.

"That is supposed to be the case, but obviously not. Watch out. Whoever they are, they're not afraid to kill whites." He paused a moment and looked around. "I'm going to requisition that wagon you mentioned, and a team to pull it."

Ben felt relieved. He was anxious to watch them leave. "No need to requisition it. I'll loan it to you."

"Whatever we choose to call it, you can retrieve it in town tonight or any time thereafter. We'll take our associate with us." He got out a fresh cigar and struck a match on the sole of his boot. He lit the cigar carefully, blew out the match and tossed it away.

CHAPTER 15

Charlie Boone had decided to go on one of his trips. Looked like they would have to leave the cave and that was an unhappy prospect because it was a comfortable place. He'd have to carry the silver with him, and he didn't like that, either, because all it would take was a pair of eyes that understood what they were seeing and no telling what might happen.

Better to move on, though. There'd be guns on the prod pretty soon and folks could get killed. The place he'd buried it was about half a morning's ride from the cave. Didn't want them red people poking around at it.

He turned in the saddle and took a long look behind. Nobody. It felt good to be alone after weeks of living hip to elbow with so many people. The trousers, shirt and boots he wore felt restrictive after going around half-naked all the time. He lifted the big sombrero and fanned himself in an absent-minded manner, watching six buzzards circle through the blue morning sky. He shifted the reins and clucked to his horse and resumed picking his way through cactus and stone.

Old Bill came to mind as he rode. All them stories. He had some all right. Funny stories that weren't all that funny if you thought about it, but you couldn't keep from laughing when he commenced one–like the time he was along with Jim Bowie and some others and Comanches ambushed 'em.

All that time under a sun just about like this one, everybody thirsty and a creek right there in sight except it was in sight of the Indians, too, and the men all scared to slip over there and bring back water.

Only one man there didn't own his own soul, Bowie tells him, *Bill, git over yonder and bring us some water.* And he done it, too, and the red men never shot at him.

Any white man would have been face down in the creek in two heartbeats, but they never harmed old Bill. Bill said the thing he remembered the rest of his life was the men drinking from the canteens he carried, their throats turned up working on that water, and not a one of them said a word of thanks.

Took a brave man. It was Charlie Boone's good luck that in his last years Bill had also been a generous man.

Once Charlie reached the hiding place it took him only a few minutes to dig up his treasure and a few more to secure it for the return journey. He let the cow pony graze while he rested in the shade, then filled his canteen from the strangled trickle of water at the base of the cliff and began the ride back.

Billings and his men had come a long way, but the sergeant continued on. He knew better than to return without some tangible result of the search. You couldn't tell what Dugan might do when he didn't get his way. This would be a good time to quit it all and just keep riding, but he knew he wouldn't. That was a coward's way, and besides, there was all that money.

The state would see very little of it. Billings had his captain's promise of a share in it and there was no way he was riding away from that. All he wanted was a stake–enough for a piece of land to raise cattle on, enough to bring his wife and boy down from Ohio.

He had watched the captain deteriorate since the end of the war. Billings and a few others were the only survivors of the company Dugan had raised and led through two years of campaigning. Once a brave and fine leader, the man was no good now. Billings had elected to follow him to Texas, lured by stories of fortunes to be made in the defeated Confederacy. Most of the stories were lies. The heat was no lie, though.

This ground they covered was too rocky for tracks. It was anybody's guess where their quarry had gone. He took off his stetson and wiped the sweat out of his eyes. A good meal would raise his spirits, he imagined, but he'd have to wait another day for that. Until then they'd live on jackrabbits and coffee.

"Sergeant." He glanced back at the voice, saw an arm pointed at something distant. Too far to tell. Might be a man on horseback. He signaled the others forward at a trot.

They began to close on the moving target and it resolved itself into a man and his horse going along at a slow walk, a near-mirage in the waves of reflected heat.

The horse stopped and they caught up to it. The rider was a negro, sweated through and through just as they were, his face shaded by a big Mexican sombrero. He rode a quarter horse whose muscular hindquarters were the sort that could jump the animal right out from under a careless rider.

If they provoked any fear in the man Billings couldn't see it. He called a halt and rode up beside Charlie, who took off his sombrero, showing a bare scalp that shone in the sun like an ebony ball. Waited for Billings to speak.

"We're state police trailing Indians that killed two of our people. You come across any?"

Charlie hesitated, then said, "Funny thing. I didn't know there was none loose til this morning, and I'm danged if they didn't come on me at breakfast. I thought I was a dead man for sure, but they just wanted some flour and coffee. I ain't got much scalp anyway, you can see."

"And what's your business out here?"

"No offense meant, but what's your business asking that question? You heard about emancipation?"

Billings ignored the question, turned in his saddle and said, "One of you search his saddlebags."

Boone got off the horse and waited for them to finish.

"Just some coffee beans, Sergeant."

"You said Indians took your coffee."

"They was accommodating Indians, mister police. Left me enough for a day or two."

"What's your destination then, somewhere close?"

Boone looked confused. "Nawsuh, I don't even know where this is. Where are we, anyhow?"

"What's your name?"

"Charlie Boone, sir. Ex-slave of the late Buford Boone of the South Carolina Boones. Trying to see the world while I'm still young."

"Get on your horse." Charlie did as the man said. "I'm taking you back to headquarters with us." If he couldn't show Dugan an Indian, at least he could bring back a man who had *seen* one.

There were objections, of course, as he expected, and there was a certain pleasure in watching fear replace the sleepy deception on Boone's face.

"Aw, sir, why you want to do that? I ain't hurt nobody. Why you take me to some jailhouse?"

"You're not under arrest. Not yet, anyway. I want my captain to hear your story." To the others he said, "Take his rifle. Keep him between two of you going back." News of turning back seemed to revive the men. They sat straighter in their saddles as they realized the hot, futile stalk had ended.

Boone continued his protests in an almost casual manner as they rode, as if he knew the complaining would do no good but had to be said anyway. But while he talked, ignoring warnings from the other horsemen, his eyes were busy mapping the countryside they traveled.

Within the hour he saw what he was looking for–a narrow arroyo cut into the earth by a hesitant run of water. The arroyo changed directions and went out of sight after fifty yards, no telling what it was like. Could be a dead end, or maybe just

86

petered out and no cover to be had, but you took what help you could get.

All the horses, including his, got their heads up approaching the wet crossing. This was thirsty country. They stayed in their seats, but let the horses drink from the shallow creek. Unlike the others, Charlie didn't let his mount fill up but pulled him back after he'd had just a little water, the horse resentful, straining against him. Belly full of water wouldn't do. There were no weapons pointed at him just now, maybe not a good chance but the best he was likely to get.

He dug both heels into the pony's flanks and bent low over the saddlehorn. The first jump got them clear and he guided the horse between the steep, sandy banks of the cut.

The first shot missed him, throwing dirt across his back. Close behind it another one hit his left stirrup and tore through his pants leg and boot. The foot went numb. He hoped the horse wasn't hit.

Almost around the bend another bullet took him in the back just as he raised up to shift his weight away from jutting rocks. The impact ripped his shirt open and knocked him flat over the saddle again. Suddenly he couldn't breathe and his eyesight narrowed to a tunnel of light in front of him. A roar filled his head like the sound of a hundred waterfalls. He held the racer's mane in one hand and planted his heels in the heaving flanks over and over and over again.

The men and their horses were tired and couldn't keep up the chase long. They'd found blood, so either horse or rider was hit, no telling how badly. Their prize had gotten away and now Billings would have to return to Dugan with nothing to show for all their effort. Ah...to blazes with Dugan. He felt too tired and hot to care.

"Sergeant?" One of his men.

"Yeah? What is it?" Billings had remained while his men chased after the fleeing Boone. In that narrow defile there wasn't room for more than two riders abreast. The trooper offered him something.

A rock? He took it in his own hand. It filled his palm, heavier than it ought to be, black with shades of gray showing through. And the shape was strange, too, thicker at the center, tapering on the ends.

"Where did you find this?"

"Right at the first bend in the creek. I saw it fall when he went around that turn."

When the others were no longer watching, Billings unfolded his knife and scraped at the thing. A bright spot of silver winked at him like a hibernating eye, freshly wakened.

If I'm dead I ain't in heaven. It's too blamed hot. The sun was on his back and his head ached and there was a throb of pain in his left heel that echoed all the way up his leg. The horse was walking, head down and reins trailing along the ground, cropping grass as he walked. Charlie was held in place by his own hand wrapped into the coarse hair of the pony's long mane. He looked around and saw nobody. His left leg dangled free, the stirrup shattered, so he dismounted on the off side. The foot hurt and his boot was mangled but he could walk on it. He checked the gelding's withers and along the ribs for sign of a wound, but found none. *Lucky horse. Lucky me.*

His shirt was torn open in back, part of it flapping in ragged tatters on his hip. That's what knocked him out, then. A slug had hit him in the back. So why was he still alive?

He unbuttoned the shirt and slipped it off and untied the canvas vest underneath and spread it open on the ground. Felt good to be free of the weight. The breeze cooled his torso, but he'd lost the sombrero and his bare head felt hammered by the sun.

The vest told the story. The bullet had hit one of the pockets and had been deflected by the ingot inside, and ripped open the pocket beside it. The silver casting had fallen somewhere behind him. Maybe they found it. He hoped not, but there was nothing to be done about it either way.

It was his good fortune they hadn't looked him over closer. He examined his left boot. The bullet that twisted his stirrup had knocked the heel off and must have taken some flesh because there was a spatter of blood on his leg. He decided to leave it be for now. The foot still had almost no feeling. Had to get moving again, the riders might still be searching for him. He patted the horse's big rump.

"You are a noble animal," he said.

Maybe they had a piece of his silver, but he had plenty, a gift from his friend. And if old Bill had told the truth there was a whole lot more of it over on the San Saba, waiting for the man who could find it.

CHAPTER 16

This was what he'd come to do. The mare was rested and ready for work and he could feel her contained energy. After a ride Hub guessed at half an hour, begun as soon as Sarah and James had left the cave shelter, he'd reached a slender creek and followed it south, leaving behind the arid, higher country, the long valleys and shimmering distances, and entered dense tangles of thorn and brier, sharp-leaved agaritas shedding their red berries among cedar and live oak that struggled to find sunlight.

Even in the shade it was no cooler in here than out in direct sunlight. No wind blew and the heat was like a wet blanket over his face as he fought through cedar needles, felt them sting his face and sift into the collar of his shirt. He had buckled on his leather chaps, but even with the chaps and the tapaderos on his stirrups the brushpopping was still hard going.

He found no cattle, not even tracks or dung, but it made sense that the herds would stay close to water and cover, so he continued south along the creek, jumping an occasional deer, and once a covey of quail exploded from underneath the mare's belly, causing horse and rider a few seconds of fright. The smell of the cedar oil on his hands from the crushed needles was clean and pleasant, but it was a relief to him when the undergrowth began to thin out and the trees became larger and wider-spaced with room to ride.

He saw more of the sky ahead through the laced branches, and fewer trees, maybe a meadow. It would feel good to ride a while without having to dodge brush and trees.

The mare's ears came up and Hub felt her muscles tense and hum along her rib cage, and just then came the sound of brush cracking, and a splash of water from the creek. He touched the horse with a boot heel and she leaped forward, mindless of herself or her rider, in pursuit.

Hub smelled the milky-sweet odor of bedded cattle as they cleared the cedar brake and burst into a meadow of tall grass hundreds of yards across. Far on the other side he caught the flash of longhorns wheeling to vanish in the trees. He got his lariat loose in two jumps and was whirling the loop, guiding the mare after a cow with a calf at her side. Catch her and the calf would stay close–two head with one throw, and he could lead her on back to Turner's.

The noose settled over the wide curl of her horns and Hub yanked back on the reins, looped the end of his rope around the saddle horn and tossed the slack line ahead. He was off the mare with a string in his hand before the cow hit the end of the rope.

The longhorn went down hard and the next moment, before sense and breath could return, Hub had her feet tied and she lay helpless, breathing hard, her eyes large and showing white, lowing to the calf in fear and surprise.

He walked up the taut rope to the mare and remounted. Halfway into the saddle he heard a bellow that wasn't calf or cow, but something wilder, full of danger and rage. He settled into the seat just as a black bull hurtled out of the cedars, paused a moment to sight on him and then came on the attack with head lowered and horns poised to kill.

The world around him slowed down as every detail showed itself like grains of sand separating in his hand. The heat of the day, the smell of horse sweat, the burn in his fingers from the rope, the black bull, not a longhorn, but a *toro*, a fighting bull, all muscle and sweep of weapon, all anger and intent. The horns looked sharp as daggers.

Hub nudged the mare a step forward, tearing the lariat free then hauling hard on the reins. They almost got away in time. He felt his seat lift as the mare's hindquarters came off the ground. She squealed when the bull's great muscular head raised and threw her off her feet. Hub fell before he could pull his revolver.

There was the quick pain of impact and he was lifted again before he got another breath, something sharp and hurtful in his thigh, whirling him in the air.

Two quick blasts of gunfire that he never heard and the ground came up and hit him a stunning blow. He tasted dirt and blood, smelled a heavy musk, tried to get to his feet but failed, and then consciousness slipped away and he was in a darkness black as the animal lying dead beside him.

Conversation. A man's laughter, the smell of coffee and the hateful, burning pain. Hub opened his eyes but was in darkness still. Was he blind? A flame stirred at the edge of his vision. A campfire. Night already? He tried to sit up but something clawed into the big muscle of his left leg and he had to give it up.

"Better be still, pardner, don't want the bleedin' to start again."

He had to twist his neck to make out the man seated beside him. Illumination from the fire was uncertain, but he appeared to be about Hub's age, dressed in rough clothing, a wild set of whiskers that needed trimming. Hub's tongue and the tissues of his lips were dry, felt swollen and unaccustomed to use. He worked his lips over his teeth and said, "My horse?"

"Well, sir, old toro got that mare of yours, too. Cut up her hind leg some." Hub groaned, not from pain, but from the frustration of his dreams. Come all this way and so close to getting the cattle he needed, and now this.

"You're lucky, though. He didn't rip her belly open like they do in them heathen bullfights. I've got her tied over yonder." He motioned with his head toward the line of dark trees. Hub wanted to see her wound, but couldn't even sit up. How had he allowed this to happen?

The stranger read his thoughts. "You couldn't of knowed there was a fightin' bull in this brush. We've seen him a time or two, but never got sights on him before. Wandered up here from somewhere down in Mexico, I reckon, and fell in love with American cows." He stopped talking, rolled and lit a cigarette. "Smoke?"

"No, thanks."

"We got some boiled beef on the fire over there."

He felt too weary to speak. He shook his head.

The stranger laughed. "It ain't that old bull. We borrowed the cow you caught."

Hub wondered about the calf, hoped it was weaned and old enough to care for itself, but he remembered it as looking very young. He wished for morning, but the pain was going to keep him awake and light would be slow coming. And then the man beside him produced a bottle, unscrewed the cap and filled a cup with liquid. He smelled whiskey. Then the man put a hand under his back and lifted him enough so that his lips could reach the offered drink.

"Swallow this down. If I can't feed you at least I can send you off to sweet dreams."

The cup tilted against his mouth and the whiskey welled out of it, harsh and full of heat. He had to swallow it, the astringent stuff burning its way down his throat. He gagged for a moment, felt as if he might drown in it, then the cup was gone and his head back on the blanket.

"Sorry to be so rough. If I let you sip it, it wouldn't do the job as fast."

It was cheap whiskey, left a taste like kerosene in his mouth and a burning in his nose and eyes, the heat of it almost painful at first, and then it leveled out and spread through him with a relief that turned warm. In a little while he closed his eyes and began to go slowly into a painless sleep.

From beside the fire one of the other men, the young one, called out, "Who is he, Raiford?"

"Don't know." He shoved himself off the ground and bent over Hub to pull up the blanket. "He ain't the law, though."

"We ought to just shoot him and be done with it."

"You're too bloodthirsty, Goose. He wasn't huntin' us. No point in takin' the man's life." He walked to the fire, brushing dead cedar needles off his pants, rearranging the stained felt hat on his head. The Mexican looked up at him from his kneeling position and handed him a cupful of the meat they had boiled for supper.

"No salt," he said.

Raiford tousled the man's black hair. "Plenty of that back in camp, Juanito. We'll have salted beef tomorrow." He cut the meat with the long blade of a folding knife and speared the pieces with its point, wiping grease off his lips with the back of his sleeve. When they finished eating the other two men put blankets down by the fire, the night turned cool now. Raiford spread his bedroll beside Hub and laid the whiskey bottle out where it was in easy reach. The *cornada* would stiffen overnight and the pain would increase.

Hub woke near dawn to the loud song of a mockingbird high in a tree, its body a gray silhouette against a lighter gray sky. The smell of whiskey was on his breath. His eyes felt sore and red from its effects, but he was grateful anyway. It had helped him get through the night and now maybe he could do something about his situation

He refused the offer of more.

The leg hurt, he couldn't deny that, and there was an ache in his shoulder like a rotten tooth, but he needed a clear head. These men gave off a scent of danger despite the care they'd provided for him. He suspected they were part of the outlaw tribes. His pants leg had been cut away, and the light from the

94

rekindled fire showed him the wound above his knee on the inside of his thigh. Could have been much worse, but there was a chance of blood poisoning if he didn't get it cared for right away.

But the mare. He had to see to her, judge for himself how badly she was hurt. Nobody else's opinion counted. "I want to try standing up," he said.

Raiford said, "That's apt to hurt."

He rolled onto his touchy shoulder and got his right knee under his body and lifted. When his head came off the ground a sea of nausea poured over him, leaving him gasping for breath, cold sweat popping out on his face. He waited for it to pass. The feeling eased a little as the world slowed its spin and he pulled himself erect with the assistance of an offered hand. This was not going to be easy.

"I whittled this thing for you." It was a long stick with a fork at the top, a sapling cut and trimmed to serve as a crutch. He smelled the sap in the fresh cuts.

"You've been a good friend. I won't forget it." A strange contrast, this man and the other two, who stayed silent and distant. He fitted the crutch under his left arm and found a way to hold himself upright. He put out his hand. "I'm Hubbard Anderson."

"Raiford Clawson. Pleased to meet you. This here's Goose and Juanito." The kid just stared. The Mexican man touched his hat brim.

Hub started toward the horses, Clawson beside him. "I put some worm medicine on it," he said. "It's all I had." Hub could see the swath of purple on her hip around the horn wound. She stood on three feet, the hind leg bent to take her weight off it.

"You led her here?"

"Yeah...well, little Juan did."

"Was she walking all right?"

"She limped, but not too bad. We thought about puttin' her down, but it ain't my business to shoot another man's horse."

"Thanks for that. This mare once saved my life. I'll save hers now." It was a long time ago, but still vivid in his mind, the long walk through the back roads of Louisiana and East Texas after the surrender, the starving horse that appeared one day and followed him down the road, refusing to leave despite the rocks and curses he threw.

Now he rubbed the mare's neck and ran a hand along her ribs. You could count these ribs from a distance back then, nothing but skin and hair covering them. Then the day when he was too starved and sick to walk any farther, but somehow pulled himself onto her back and hung there like a corpse while she carried him home.

They'd been together so long he couldn't imagine life without this horse, but this had been a close one. And not over yet.

"I'll put her down for you." The lazy words were accompanied by the cocking of a hammer behind him.

"Put that thing back in your holster, Goose. Ain't nobody wants this horse put down."

"Got to be done, Raiford. Can't let a dumb animal suffer." Hub couldn't see the boy's eyes, but sensed a gleam in them. Here was a young man who liked to hurt things. Hub's gunbelt was somewhere else. All he had was the wooden crutch.

"You shoot this horse, you'll have to shoot me, too, because I'll kill you for it, mister."

"Oh, yeah?" The barrel shifted to the center of Hub's chest. "I don't mind that, neither."

CHAPTER 17

Raiford Clawson's hand came out of the dark and clamped down between the hammer and firing pin of Goose's pistol and in the same motion twisted the weapon out of the boy's grasp then hit him with the butt of it, knocking him to his knees.

Clawson let the hammer gently down and stuck the pistol in the front of his pants.

"Give my gun back, Raiford."

"You can have it after while, Goose, when you calm down some. And maybe then you can just ride on back to Missouri. What do you think?"

The boy's voice was almost a whine. "I want to stay with you and Juan." The blow had left a shallow cut in his hairline. He wiped at it and left a smear of blood on his jaw.

"You got to behave proper, then. Now, go get you some coffee." Raiford extended a hand and helped him up.

"All right, but you hurt me with that durn gun." He went slowly back to the fire and poured himself a cup. The Mexican man had watched it all without interest.

Raiford said to Hub, "You live close?"

"No, I'm from over in the Brazos valley." He could feel the muscles of his body begin to loosen, the reaction to Goose's threat drift away. "I'm trying to catch some cows is all."

"Well, I was you I'd find me a doctor to look at that leg."

Hub said, "There's a ranch east of here. They'll help me if I can just get there."

Raiford gave it some thought, turned around and walked halfway back toward the fire. "I'm gonna help this man get where he wants to go," he called. "You go on back to camp and I'll meet you later on."

Neither of the men liked the news. Goose argued with him, demanded the pistol again, but he just shook his head and came back to Hub.

"I'll ride you up behind me and we'll lead the mare. That sound okay to you?"

"I hate to impose, especially at the cost of trouble between you and your friends. I can see they don't agree with you."

"Why, Goose don't ever agree to nothing. He'd argue with Saint Peter at the gate of Heaven." They got the horses ready and left in a few minutes as the sun climbed higher and brought the full morning to light. Hub worried a little about showing Clawson where the Turners lived, but the man seemed decent and he'd just have to hope nothing bad came of it, because he had no real choice.

The mare limped, but she would make the trip without too much trouble.   They passed the body of the black bull, already beginning to bloat in the heat, buzzards circling overhead. This was the last thing he'd wanted. And now he faced, how long? A week? Maybe longer, without a cow in the pen. He had arrived with a plan and some hope, but fate kept dealing him unlucky hands. He moved the injured leg to a better position.

His luck would turn. It always had and would again.

Clawson was an interesting man, but he didn't give much of himself away. Hub would've like to ask him a few questions, find our more, but that wasn't something you did out here. People went their own way and could get deadly mean at too many questions.

They traveled slow. The mare's every step caused her

obvious pain. They stopped often to let her rest and when they reached a stream of water later in the morning Clawson got down and helped Hub off the horse and let the animals graze in the tall grass that grew there. The two men sat in silence for long moments after they drank their fill. Crows fought in a cottonwood a hundred yards downstream, dragonflies hovered along the winding waterway. The shade was cool.

"I'm tryin' to recall," Clawson said after awhile, "if I ever thought this much of any horse I have rode, and I believe the answer is, I have not." Hub realized it was an invitation to talk. Curiosity ran both ways.

He told him the story.

"A sentimental man. I saved the life of a sentimental man."

Hub laughed at him, but his leg pained so much he wondered if he'd be able to ride the rest of the way. Clawson had a question.

"You fight in Pennsylvania?"

"No. My brother did, though. Killed at Gettysburg."

"Well, now. Sorry to hear it. I was right there, too. In that fool charge we made–don't know why they called it *Pickett's Charge*. Pickett didn't want it. Nobody wanted it but Bobby Lee, and he acourse got to watch from a safe distance." He threw a stone at the creek.

Ben Turner's horse pasture lay to the northwest of his house, twenty acres more or less, fenced with stone horse-high, a project that had taken Ben and all the labor he could hire nearly half a year of hard work to complete. The pasture was meadow, cleared out of the denser forest that was its northern boundary. They left a few of the larger cedars and all the hardwoods, oak and a few elms for shade, the other brush chopped out and burned to make room for the grasses that filled it now. On the other side of its west fence the trees and thorn scrub grew dense again, interspersed with small natural clearings used as bedding places by deer and cattle, connected by narrow trails where red sand and caliche showed through the sparse grass, compacted by the almost daily tread of hooves.

There was a mighty lot of travel in these hills today. They'd already had to skirt around a band of armed riders who looked dirty and tired, coming back toward the Llano. Now here was another bunch. Raiford threw his hat in the grass where Hub was resting. Clawson's horse was grazing, but the mare simply stood with her bad leg cocked so that the other three legs held her weight. They were safe and out of sight in the trees and could see down a slight rise to the house where people and horses were moving around.

Raiford watched an older man with one arm walk into the pasture below and round up a mule and white pony and lead them out. A few minutes later the animals appeared again, now hitched to a wagon that hauled what looked to be a man. The whole mess of them rode away, wagon and all, with the one-armed man watching them go. That must be Turner.

He'd been right not to go riding in there without a good look-see. Wouldn't hurt to wait a little longer, either. Anderson was asleep or maybe unconscious, and Raiford was tempted to just leave him and the horse right there. He had already played the Good Samaritan, why not get up and go? The man could find his own way from here.

It wouldn't do to run into lawmen without Goose and Juanito to back him. Then again, Missouri was a long way off. Probably nobody in these woods ever heard of them.

Hub solved his problem by waking up. He got upright with the usual struggle, his hair tangled with dry grass and his face as pale as a sun-bleached bone.

"What is it?"

"Aw, some people at the house yonder. Left just now pullin' a wagon."

Hub thought about it with the buzz of fever in his ears. Probably Dugan. They found the wounded man–or maybe he was dead by now. They took Ben's wagon to carry him back to town. He kept his thoughts to himself.

"It'll be just Ben Turner and his daughter down there now,"

he said, and wondered if he was trusting this Clawson too much. He could see reluctance in the man's face and he could imagine the reasons why.

Ben thought at first that Dugan and his men had returned when he heard the dog bark again, then the sound of horses and a voice calling out.

"Our day for visitors," he said. Sarah had come out of her bedroom, depression and fear evident in the sag of her shoulders. She'd purposely left the dried blood on her cheeks overnight for reasons that seemed less important now. She went to the wash basin on the back porch and scrubbed her face, ignoring the sting of the water, and toweled herself dry.

When her father went outside she followed and was surprised to find Hubbard Anderson on a makeshift crutch, helped along by a disreputable-looking stranger. Her thoughts went straight as an arrow to her son. "Johnny?..." she started, but Hub was shaking his head and the question trailed away unfinished.

"Just me," he said. "Bull gored me." The pain was evident in the set of his mouth, the clenched jaw. She led them through the house to the room where John slept and helped get him into the bed. She put a folded sheet under the wounded leg to soak up any bleeding, took a pair of scissors to the rough bandage Raiford had put there and exposed the crusted tear. She heard Ben whistle in sympathy.

"Now, that hurts a man. I've seen a few in my time."

The stranger said, "I witnessed the tangle and I can tell you this boy and his mare come off a sight better than I expected."

Ben looked around. "I'd better see about the horse."

"I'll come out there, too, you don't mind." He followed. Sarah imagined the man spent his time out of doors. He could do with a wash, and there was a quality in his bearing that seemed out of place among floor rugs and doilies. A hard man, probably, but with compassion that seemed almost out of character.

Hub read her thoughts. "His name's Raiford Clawson. Saved

my life."

"Yes," she said, "I think he did."

"There's other men out there now," he said. "I hate to alarm you but it looked like they were coming from the north, but didn't look like they found anything. Manning alive?"

"Yes. They came for him earlier. He's maybe already told them what happened. I don't know what to do, and now here you are..."

"Sarah, I'll go somewhere else if I'm in the way here. I just didn't know what else..."

"No, no no, I didn't mean to imply ...I have to get back to them, that's all. Johnny's expecting to hear from me."

"Ben gonna let 'em come?"

"Well, he didn't like the idea, but this is my home, too. I'll change his mind."

"How about James? He could ride back."

"No, I'm the one going, just as soon as I can."

"Sarah..."

"Hush." She got soap and water and washed the wound and put iodine on it and bound it with clean cloth. Then combed his red hair clean of the burrs and bits of grass. He was lean and hard, the muscles of his body alive when he moved. The stink of dried sweat drifted off his clothing and skin. *He should be washed,* she thought, and felt a surprising response to the image, a sweep of fingers across the tight strings of a well-tuned guitar.

The horse would heal up if the wound didn't get infected and if he could keep the worms out of it. The mare was out to pasture for a while. Ben watched Raiford finish the bacon and biscuits Sarah had put away after their own meal. The stranger scraped a shred of meat from between his teeth with a fingernail and said, "Maybe I'll ask you a favor if you don't mind."

"What's that?"

"Just, if them people come back out here, leave off telling

about me."

"You've got my word on it. I'll mention it to my daughter, too."

Sarah came into the kitchen as the two stood. "I'm much obliged for the meal," the tall man said.

Ben said, "You must be tired. You're welcome to stay the night. Plenty of beds in the bunkhouse."

But he was already moving for the door. "Thanks aplenty, Mr. Turner, and ma'am, but I better go on. There's friends waiting on me." They went into the yard with him and watched him mount up. Sarah said, "Thank you for your help." He unwrapped his gunbelt from the horn and buckled it around his waist, touched the brim of his hat and in minutes was out of sight.

"Did you ask his name?" She said.

"No, I believe he's on the run. Got that look about him."

The two of them fought that night. Ben had never seen her like this before, nearly crazed with worry for the boy, something bold in her blood almost out of control.

"I must go!" She said. "Either tonight or in the morning. And I will bring them here. He won't leave that girl, and there's no other hope of keeping him out of Dugan's hands."

"Sarah, we don't know for sure if Manning has said anything. He wasn't talking when I last saw him. But I don't know but one way to find out. In the morning I'll go in for the wagon. Then we'll know and we can make up our minds what to do."

"It doesn't matter. I'm going back for him."

Ben took her arm. "You'll stay with Hub while I go to town in the morning. I'm an old man, Sarah. My hair is white and one arm is gone and I creak a little when I walk, but I am still a man and I won't sit here and watch you ride off into rough country alone. So just for now, you act like a woman. And let me do the sort of thing I've done all my life."

CHAPTER 18

Ben spent an uneasy night and was on horseback well before dawn, nothing but coffee for his breakfast. It seemed strange that the town was just waking up and getting about its business. Worried that the story had already spread, he forced himself to enter Dugan's office, expecting to find the tyrannical man behind his desk. Empty. A footstep behind him.

"You ain't supposed to be in here, mister." Cooter had a broom in his hand.

"Sorry. I'm looking for your captain."

"He'll be over at the saloon, but I wouldn't bother him if I was you."

"He took my wagon to bring in your wounded man yesterday. Said I could pick it up this morning."

"Oh, you're Mr. Turner. The wagon's out back and I got your team penned at the foot of the hill. I'll help you get 'em."

"How is your patient today?"

"You mean Leo? Well, it looks like he'll live, though that may not be what you'd care to hear."

Ben felt a sting of apprehension. "What do you mean?"

Cooter seemed embarrassed. "Oh, I just meant about him

fighting with your boy the other day. He can be awful rough."

"Is he awake yet? Talking?" Ben's tongue felt thick and dry when he asked the question.

"No, I got him on a cot in the back so I can keep an eye on him, but he ain't had much to say, I reckon. Just lays there asleep."

So it was all still up in the air, and there was time to do something. What, he didn't know. They hitched the team to his wagon. Ben tied the pinto's reins to the back and climbed up on the seat. The team had rested and fed well overnight, and they pulled him down the nearly empty street at a quick pace until he recognized James Harper standing outside his store and waving him down.

He told James about Hub's injury and couldn't miss the quick shadow of jealousy on the man's face.

"I'll ride out tomorrow and see him if you don't mind."

"Glad to have you." It was the courteous thing to say, though not true this time. Harper was a good man, but too much was going on for them to worry about his jealousy. And it might get worse, because there was a change in Sarah. A change that would be good for her, he thought, but maybe not for the good of Harper. Not even for the good of Ben Turner. He leaned closer.

"Manning still has not told anything. Maybe you can find out how he is before you come. If he's repeated what he said out there."

James glanced across the street. Figures moved inside the saloon. "I'll do that, Ben. And I'll come sooner if the news is bad."

Ben lifted his hat, wiped sweat off his forehead with his shirt sleeve, replaced the hat, gave James a quick nod, slapped the reins on the animal's rumps and continued downhill to the river.

On a cot in the back of the log building a mind swam up from somewhere dark and deep. He had been a long time getting here, skipping like a flat stone over bright water, dark and then light and then dark again as the pain rose and fell. But he could take in air and breathe it out, and so he must still contain life. He cast about for familiar feelings, well-known patterns. Manning opened his eyes, and for the first time in what might have been a thousand years, knew where he was, knew who he was.

He searched far inside himself for the rage that had always filled him in a more satisfying way than food or whiskey or even the love of a woman ever had. He couldn't locate it, but it would come. He was alone, and that was all right, too. He had always been alone, even among the other men.

There was a stink in his nose and he knew it was his own breath. His face felt stiff as starched cloth and his whiskers were long and dense. He imagined how bad he must look.

He smiled.

Sergeant Lawrence Billings was slow to leave the barracks this morning. He was of two minds. On the one hand it would mollify Dugan if he turned over the silver thing. Deflect the criticism that was sure to come after losing the prisoner. On the other hand, Dugan would take it over, and if there was meaning in it, a chance at more like it, he would take that over, too.

Might be wise to ask around a little. Surely somebody knew. He took the object out of his pocket and looked at it again. The way it tapered down on two sides it looked almost like...well, like a lizard.

Billings was not a stupid man. Nor was he ignorant. His rise in rank during the war proved it. But he was a man of the North. His family still farmed the soil of Ohio and frequent letters begged him to come home. The reason he had stayed was the same reason he had followed Dugan here in the first place–the chance to make money. But so far all he had to show for the effort were the promises Dugan dropped now and then like crumbs from his table.

After all, he knew the direction the rider had come from even if he didn't know where he was headed. He knew what the man looked like. He knew his name. This belonged to Billings. He made up his mind.

The store owner was a Texan, had lived around here all his life. Maybe he knew something. Couldn't show it to him, no. Just approach the subject casual-like, a conversation, idle curiosity. He walked to the store. There was s customer inside, a teamster from the sound of their talk. Billings turned his back to the men and pretended to look over merchandise until the teamster finished his business and left.

"Help you?" Harper didn't sound friendly. Nobody around these parts was friendly when they talked to Dugan's men. Billings cared little, one way or the other.

"I need some shells for my rifle," he said.

"Don't you draw your ammunition at your barracks? I believe you're well supplied."

He'd expected the question. "Well, I had a run in with a couple of the men this morning. I'd as soon not go back til the air clears a little. You know what I mean."

"Sure, I guess I do. Want a box?"

"That'll be fine." While James got the cartridges the sergeant leaned against the counter and then, as though it had just occurred to him, said "You're a man that can maybe settle a question's been worrying me for days."

"What's that?" James put the box down and waved off the offer of money. "I'll add it to Dugan's account."

"Obliged. Well, on the street the other day I heard two men talking and it seemed like one of them had found something out in the hills that had him wondering. What he told the other one was that it was a piece of silver that looked like it was molded into a shape."

"Oh yeah?" James was interested now, all right. Comes to treasure, every man gets a light in his eye.

"He said it looked to him kind of like a lizard. You ever hear such as that?"

James focused all his attention on him now. "A silver lizard?

Who was the man?"

"Don't know. Stranger to me, and I didn't want to nose in, but I couldn't stop thinking about it."

"No offense, Sergeant, but this is hard to believe." Billings remained silent. "There's a story–a myth, a legend, call it what you want, about *Las Iguanas,* a silver mine in early Spanish Texas over on the San Saba River. Story goes the Spaniards mined silver close to their mission and made it into ingots shaped like iguanas. Shipped them down the river to the Gulf and then on to Spain."

Billings had to work at keeping his hands still, his face noncommittal. This was no myth. He was one of maybe two men who knew it was a certainty. "What happened to it? I mean, what's *supposed* to've happened to it?"

"Well, as best I remember the local Indians got tired of it all and massacred everybody and took the treasure and sealed it up in a cave."

"That's some story, all right. And I reckon it ain't been seen since?"

"There's a second part to the story. People claimed Jim Bowie found it just before he died at the Alamo and never told anybody else where it was. I guess that's a convenient way to end a legend. But you say some man talked about finding one of those ingots."

"That's what I heard him say, all right." Billings had to get out of there. "Understand now, I'm staking no claim to the truth of it. But no matter, I've got work to do and had better get along to it."

It was a discomfort, knowing James watched him as he went out the door, knowing he'd overstepped a little, raised interest in something that had to be kept secret. But at least now he knew. There was a real treasure somewhere in these forsaken hills. Let Dugan keep his crumbs. Lawrence Billings would make his own future. Without asking Dugan's permission, telling no one, he saddled his horse and put together a few necessaries and rode out of town.

Three dusty riders passed him on the street near the saloon where a piano played already, a tune that sounded like mice running on the keys. They were well-armed men and he called out to them, "You gentlemen leave your sidearms in your saddlebags while you're in town." He laughed to himself at this habitual show of authority. There was a chance he wasn't even coming back here.

Raiford Clawson offered him a compliant wave and a smile. The man had a badge on his shirt, and anyway it was no problem. Raiford and Goose each had boot guns and they had not come looking for any trouble. If the need arose Juan Rivera would make do with his long, thin Arkansas Toothpick, strapped to his back in such a way that the handle rode just beneath the collar of his shirt and could be extracted from its sheath and put into action faster than any gun.

The saloon was cool inside. Or at least it was not as hot as the street or the cedar brakes they'd ridden through to get here. A skinny man with a derby hat on his head sat at a piano in the corner. A game of poker was going on at a table, four men bent over their cards. Tobacco smoke and alcohol were what you breathed in here, like any saloon, and there seemed to be a leftover smell of fried bacon in the air. It was too hot for whiskey. They ordered draft beer at the bar and stood drinking it.

When they finished, Raiford called the barkeeper over and handed him a sealed envelope. "I was asked to turn this over to you for Jezzie," he said. "Can you see she gets it?"

"Yessir, be happy to." Raiford overpaid him for the beer. They rode the street all the way to its end. Then back toward the river again, stopping off at Harper's store to buy a few supplies–a sack of pinto beans, a sack of flour and enough smoking tobacco to last a few days. Goose preferred a chew, but he had plenty. They'd come on a long ride and spent less than an hour in town, but they left with everything they needed.

When they quit the trail a few miles from town they paid no attention to the single set of fresh hoof prints that continued west.

Lawrence Billings had brought supplies for three days. There was food in his saddlebags and two canteens of water and enough ammunition to hold off half the Comanche nation. Twilight had begun settling in when he recognized the little creek across the trail and the big, sandy banks farther over. It was there that the silver piece had fallen. He made a tiny fire for coffee and put his bedroll under a stunted cypress. While there was still light he walked a mile or more down the creekbed, searching among the torn tracks of horses and among the rocks as if they might release a secret. Or another silver winking eye. He found nothing.

CHAPTER 19

The street beneath her window was practically empty. Jezzie sat down to apply her makeup before the mirror just as she did every morning. Of course, it wasn't morning anywhere else–the day was well advanced–but her life ran on a different clock. *Her* clock. She didn't rush the days or the nights, not since Emil Dugan had shined on her and began to share everything but his thoughts. So Raif got her letter. And wasn't it just like him to show up and never a word said? She looked at the piece of paper again, something torn out of a child's school tablet, no explanation, just the pencil-drawn map with an X near what looked like the road west from the river junction. And *RAIFORD* printed in block letters across the bottom.

Notes from the piano below squeezed through the thin wooden floor. She was sick of the noise. Music was all right when you were up and having fun, but half the night? *All* night sometimes when business was good. She sighed.

Now that he was here they'd have to be careful nobody connected them. When would she ride out to find him? Tomorrow would be best, and she'd better get up before noon to take care of it. Something else had Dugan's attention anyhow. He wouldn't tell her what it was, but all through supper the night before he'd been unusually quiet, none of his bragging stories, almost courteous to the man who brought their food. Not himself at all. How much was in that chest anyway? When she asked him he would only say, *a great deal, my dear.*

She dabbed perfume behind her ears and waited while it dried.

Morning came again. Billings drank his coffee and debated his direction. He could either continue to the point where they'd come onto Boone, then attempt to track him in reverse to the source of the silver, or follow his trail from here–try to run him down. The man had been hit, could be he was hurt, laying up somewhere. It made sense to play it that way, didn't it? He rolled a smoke and lit it, saddled his horse and a few minutes later began to follow the arroyo.

The sun had not yet burned off the morning dew when he came across the spot where Charlie had regained consciousness and gotten down off the quarter horse. The grass was depressed–something had bent it down, and Charlie had walked around the horse, probably checking for bullet wounds. Apparently there were none, no sign of blood on the trail all morning. Billings figured he hadn't been hurt after all, wasn't hiding out or wounded, and had probably already made good time away from this place. He lost the tracks on rocky ground, then found them again at a stream crossing, and that was the pattern of the day until they disappeared altogether at last and never showed again no matter how many times he circled through the countryside.

He lay beside his fire that evening holding the iguana in his hand, feeling its weight, stroking it lightly with the blade of his knife so that it shone more and more as he carefully scraped away the patina of centuries.

Miles away Emil Dugan had spent the day in a quiet fury,

watching for his sergeant's return from whatever journey he'd undertaken without permission, without authorization, without so much as a report on his last scouting detail.

Dugan had questioned the men who'd accompanied Billings on that scout and learned upsetting things. Had Billings thought no one would notice that what fell from the fugitive horseman was strange? Heavy? Something the sergeant hadn't reported.

"I can't swear to it, Captain," the man had told him, "but it looked to me like tarnished silver."

Silver? Where was it, then, and where was Billings? And where was that black traveler?"

Those were the questions all right. The riddle. Had Billings gone off on his own to solve it? Never mind that Dugan had promised to share his treasure, never mind that he'd brought the man with him to share in whatever wealth they could uncover in this backward country.

No, on the strength of some pipedream the sergeant had turned on him, turned on his mentor, as though Dugan had no feelings, and no rights either. Every man for himself? Very well, so be it. The foolish sergeant would regret his actions.

No good to sit and think about the deception. It only made his chest hurt and the muscles of his neck and shoulders tighten into knots. At least the traitor had kept it to himself. The other men could only guess.

But Dugan knew very well Lawrence Billings would never risk his share of the treasure chest for anything less than great wealth. Correction–the *possibility* of great wealth. There was no air of gossip among the others that he could detect, and he considered himself a leader with a keen perception of such things. He left the desk and felt better stretching his legs, moving, walking. He would work it out, the answer would come to him. It always did.

He walked into the back portion of the building. The Cooter fellow seemed flustered by his appearance, but no matter. He asked to see the recovering man.

Leo Manning was not so huge a presence now. Much of the

fat that hung on him had drained away during the time he'd lain close to death, unable to eat. But now here he was sitting up on the edge of the bed with his feet on the floor.

"You look much better."

"Yes, sir, reckon I am." His voice was reedy, weak. "I do feel stronger. Can't stand up, though. I just got through trying and it didn't work."

There was a stink in the air back here. Dugan supposed it was a combination of human waste and the breath from lungs not yet healed. He tried to ignore it. "Perhaps next time. Eat the food they bring you. That's important."

Manning lay back on the cot.

"Can you tell me what happened?" This had been a great irritation–his inability to find out anything from the surviving trooper.

Manning shook his head. "I'm blank, sir. We left town on patrol and after that I just don't know."

"All right. I expect it will come to you. Rest and eat your food. We'll talk again."

"Yes, sir. Thank you, sir."

For a moment Dugan would have sworn he detected evasion in the man's countenance. But no, Manning was a loyal if mindless bull. Deception required a brain.

His leg hurt all right, but it wasn't as bad as it could have been. Hubbard walked from the bedroom to the kitchen where the others sat arguing over coffee. He limped. There was no fever, though. Sometime in the night he'd come out of a formless dream covered in sweat, his face cool and a thirst in him so powerful he had forced himself through the dark house to the water bucket and consumed three dippers full.

Two days as an invalid and he had reached his limit.

It was plain in their faces they didn't want him in here, but back behind the bedroom door under a blanket. He pulled out a chair anyway and sat down, looked with a certain amount of longing at their cups. Sarah got up and poured one for him.

"You should be in bed," she said. He shook his head silently. At first the coffee seemed acidic, burned his tongue as he swallowed. The second sip was better.

James was there, seemed friendly enough but reserved and careful. James said, "I suppose it's true, but even so, who's to say when his memory will come back?"

Hub said, "Manning?"

James nodded. "He don't remember anything, is what they told me." Hub remained silent after the news. More and more this seemed to be something that was no longer his business. Ben regarded him.

"When do you think you'll be fit to ride again?"

"I'm not sure," he said. "A day or two."

"You and me's got unfinished business yet, don't we?"

Hub had wondered about that, had been too shy to ask if Ben still wanted to partner with him. He smiled. "It's all still to do. Haven't looked at my mare yet, though. How is she?"

Ben said, "A little sore, like you, but she's walking good. I'd say let's give you both another three days and then see if we can't get some bovines in the pen."

"Three days? Sounds like three years to me. But you're right."

Sarah said, "Please be careful. If you open that wound up again, you'll just have to get off your feet and wait some more."

They made their plans and he listened, nothing to say about it–didn't want any say in it. He knew part of the way he felt was just left over from the fever, but he had stepped in a boghole, all right. He cared as much as the next man, he supposed, about the welfare of the boy and the Comanches, but his own business was still undone, not even started if you wanted to look at it that way. It was past time for him to get busy, and he was more frustrated with every passing minute.

James and Sarah were heading back to the hiding place to find her son and bring them all back to this ranch, hide them here until they could figure out what to do with them next.

There was no guarantee the Indians would even come, of course. If not, would John? No one could say. They would have to go and find out. Ben would stay here with Hub.

He silently sipped his coffee, enjoying the taste now, the warmth of it sliding down his throat, thinking of the bull and the very close encounter he'd had with death. That dark, musky smell. The waste of it.

The three days were slow in passing. He was out of the bed and fully dressed in two, but the limp was there, and a pain when he walked that he wouldn't admit. The mare seemed stiff in the leg, but the cut had almost healed and he figured gentle exercise was the best thing for them both so he led her a few miles on the trail to town, ignoring Ben's protests, and he was right. The stiffness seemed to work its way out of her. He felt better, too, after the walk. A week in bed was too much for him to handle. On the third day he followed the same routine and had good results again. The day had almost ended when the two riders appeared in the distance. Hub and Ben were watching for them.

They rode to the porch and sat their horses. There was a weariness about them, a defeat in their faces. Sarah said, "They're gone."

CHAPTER 20

Charlie Boone rode in front. They had finally reached country John claimed to know well, so Boone could relax a little, let his horse drift back some while John pointed them home. Charlie had brought them on a crazy, meandering journey, wasting miles and time because he was afraid somebody might be tracking him, might have found the silver piece back there, might already be in the cave beginning to figure things out. Nobody would be on them now, though–they'd covered their tracks too well. And the vest, with its silver ingots, was buried again, where he could find it easily enough when he needed it.

Question was, would Turner let them stay at his ranch place. The boy claimed to believe so, and there didn't seem to be any other place for them right now. Pity about the old man they had left behind, wounded and all like he was, and the young man, too, Falling Rock's boy, both of them split off now and determined to find a wild band still free. Keep on fighting. You couldn't make a Comanche do what he didn't want to do. Charlie had warned them someone was liable to come along, so maybe they had left the cave by now.

I ought to go on somewhere else, myself. But it didn't feel right. He was used to being around folks again. That old lonesome trail had lost a bunch of shine. Just have to wait and see. Could be he'd move on anyway. Maybe this place ahead would be too much like a plantation. Big house on big land.

Cattle instead of cotton. The old thoughts drifted in. The old memories. He tried to put his mind on other things. Those old memories had too much power, could fill him up with anger or sadness, make him weak and sick sometimes. Crazy.

The planters had been leaching the life from the soil of Boone Prairie for a hundred years when Charlie was born. When Buford was born. One to inherit its sorrows, one to die young defending what could not be defended.

The boys played in the dirt together as children, then Charlie was old enough and strong enough to pull a sack down the long cotton rows and for him play ceased forever. He saw his mother at night, not mornings, because she went early to the big house to help prepare the white people's breakfast. He followed his father into the field with a hoecake in his hand.

His escape from hard labor came about the time his voice changed, when his mother discovered a houseboy was needed and brought Charlie for old man Boone's inspection.

He wore their funny little britches, and he bowed and scraped and smiled. He would have sung songs if that's what they'd wanted, because he was out of the fields. And he got to spend time with Buford again. *Fetch this for me. Get that clean.* Learned manners, the placement of plates and cups and spoons.

Then the dying started. His mother, Master Boone. A year later his father, using the last of his breath urging Charlie to find a way off that place. *Run* was the last word he whispered.

But it was too late, because by then Charlie had begun loving Rosabelle, the pretty young girl who helped out in the kitchen, and running would have meant leaving her behind. Time went by and he got old enough and tall enough and he married her and they spent their days seeing after Buford and the old lady who never left her upstairs room, and their nights together in the shack that was their home.

The trouble started when Buford brought his bride to the mansion. Hair like the cotton they grew, face pale, no heart, no heart whatsoever. They worked doubly hard to make her happy, but she never was, and she developed a dislike for Rosabelle, though she never said why.

Buford went to war. The old lady died.

Word came the next summer that Buford had taken a yankee bullet, and just like that, quick as you could tell it, Charlie and Rosabelle and their baby boy so new he didn't yet have a name, became the sudden chattel of Abigail Boone, nee Fuller, of Charleston.

That day...that *particular* day, the overseer, man by the name of Boggs, and two others caught hold of Charlie and tied him with chains to the whipping post out back of the big house and wouldn't answer him when he begged to know what it was for. As it turned out, they didn't whip him.

A wagon came, pulled by two gray mules. An ugly white man wearing a derby hat and dressed in ragged clothes drove the team, and beside him on the seat was another white man, this one bigger and dressed better, puffing a cigar and blowing off smoke in big clouds between clenched teeth. He heard screams from the cabins, tore at the chains until his hands bled. *What? What are they doing?*

They brought Jasper out. His legs went bad a year before and he wasn't any help in the fields now. And Toby, just a boy but already run off twice.

And Rosabelle and the baby.

Left him chained to the post all day and night and the next day, too. Someone put a jug of water within reach. He broke it against the post and would have used a sharp fragment to cut his own throat, but Boggs had been thinking of that and they got it away from him in time.

Then they whipped him.

A taste of what will happen if you run away. *Where are they?* Dead. To you.

He meant to go. Some night, some noon, into the unknown

world. He meant to go but did not and time passed.

The war ended and some soldiers in blue said he was free now. No man's slave. The army set up a big camp, great canvas tents, herds of horses and mules, too many soldiers to count idling the days away at Boone Prairie.

On one of those days he slipped into a tent and came out carrying a loaded revolver and a belt of cartridges.

He didn't shoot Boggs. "I never wanted to do them things to you, Charlie."

The woman had fled to Charleston. "I don't know who it was she sold 'em to."

He cut the man's throat instead with a butcher knife from the kitchen and stole his horse and in three days reached the Fuller house in Charleston. Boggs' clothes didn't fit him well but they looked all right. Blood had caked on his right hand, the knife hand, and he was careful not to wash it off. Somehow it helped to calm him knowing it was there, turning hard and brown and sticking tightly to his skin.

Two days of careful watching and there she was at last, in a one-horse covered buggy driven by a black man in funny britches who must have missed the news that he was free. Charlie caught up with them on Boggs' horse at a stretch of road without houses, showed the driver his pistol and directed him to drive the buggy into a copse of trees that hid them well enough.

"Scream, miz Boone, and I'll shoot you." She must have believed him because she only stared into his eyes quietly.

To the driver he said, "Don't you know you free?"

"I always been here."

"You git on. I need to talk to her, but you go on."

"Don't you hurt her none."

"Git on. Don't send nobody else neither. I'll shoot her if you do."

The man walked away, glancing back with wide eyes shining white in his face. Charlie said, "Where is Rosabelle and my baby?"

Her face was pale as ever, but she showed little fear. Even with the gun he was not a man in her eyes and the knowledge made him angrier still.

"I sold them to Rafter in New Orleans."

"What he do with them?"

A shrug. "I don't know." It was a sorrowful thing to hear, but he had expected it. The woman considered it a victory. He could tell by the uncertain smile at the corners of her ugly, pale lips.

Shouts down the street. The stupid man. He had gone for help. Abigail heard them, too, and her face was full of satisfaction. A red mark appeared on her forehead. Something stained her dress. Charlie thought *no*. The buck of the pistol tore it loose from his grip and he had to jump off the horse to get it, thinking all the time, *did I do that?* With his ears ringing from the blast.

He remounted. People came running and all he could do was charge through them. They moved out of his path, their mouths opened in round, pink circles and their faces sharp as broken glass with surprise and a lack of understanding. *I didn't mean it,* was the thought in his head over and over, riding away, and then after a time, weaving its way between the sounds of hoofbeats, another thought came–*yes I did. Yes, I did.*

He would hang for the killings if they caught him, but he no longer cared. He rode faster than any news that might be on his heels. The fact that he didn't care if he was caught, didn't care if he was hanged, but rather welcomed the idea of death as an end to his misery, seemed to make him invisible. Nobody looked at him. Nobody cared who he was or why he had come when he at last entered New Orleans.

The trip was for nothing.

The yankees had long since closed down the slave trader Amos Rafter. The building that had once housed his trade was boarded up. Charlie wandered the city for days, part of a black tide that moved one direction for a time, then the other, an aimless, fearful, hungry mass. He mentioned the Boone name, he asked about a woman and baby son, about the hated Rafter. *No. No. Can't help you.*

For two days he lived on a dozen sausage links he got in trade for the horse. The gun and knife he kept inside his clothing, slept at night wherever he could hide. Thoughts of his own death were sweet, but he wished that he might know, before his own end, into what hell they had sent his woman and child.

He was on a pier that extended over the water like a dirty tongue, its boards rotted half away, creaking under his feet. Why had he come here? His mind was sluggish and uncertain. To jump into the water? That must be it. Or to decide about it anyway, make up his mind if that was what he should do.

Two young white boys dangled lines on cane poles. Their corks lifted and dropped in the constant movement of the water. A black man sat there, too, at a distance from the boys. He wore a ragged straw hat. His pole was a slender sapling. Something pulled his cork under and he lifted a small fish that struggled on the boards making a loud croaking noise until the fisherman removed the hook and threaded the fish on a stringer with others he'd caught and dropped them back in the water.

"What kind of fish is that?" Charlie asked him.

"Call that a Croaker," the man said, looking at him for the first time. But he didn't look away. He wasn't as old as Charlie had thought, more of a boy, and strange, too, because he kept on staring.

"Charlie? Ain't you Charlie?"

First it scared him. Had news of murder caught up to him after all? But the face was familiar.

"Don't you know me, Charlie? I'm Toby. Toby."

From the trader's Toby had gone to a German widow by the name of Leverkuhn. Though he had been filled with hatred and the urge to run again, the old lady had treated him kindly and after a while it seemed better to just stay put. She had taught him to read words in her Bible and to write his name. Now she was old, sometimes hungry, her wealth gone. There was nobody else to care for her. The fish were for her supper.

Charlie said, "What about your own mama and daddy? Who is it taking care of them?"

"Have you seen 'em?"

"Yes, I have. Your sister, too. They all still at Boone Prairie when I left."

"Maybe I'll ask miz Leverkuhn to let me go see about them. She ought not to mind."

"Toby, you don't have to ask nobody. You free to go. Don't you understand that?"

Toby seemed troubled by the words. "No. I hear you, but no, I don't understand none of it." And after a silence, "I seen the man bought Rosabelle and your boy."

Something sucked all the air out of Charlie and he could not hear the sound of his own voice. "You seen him? You know his name?"

"Ain't never heard no name. miz Leverkuhn didn't know it. Said he was from Texas, though. A preacher."

"They went to Texas?"

"Reckon they did, Charlie. She named the baby before they sold us. He's Tom, she told me. Tom. That's your boy."

Charlie fought the mosquitoes and lived on squirrels and snake meat through the Atchafalaya, stayed a few weeks with renegades called theirselves *Seminole*. Indians and runaway slaves living together way off in the swamps, hardly knew about the war, didn't know freedom had come, so Charlie was the messenger who spread the word.

Gave him his taste for the red man's ways and he carried it along while he went on into Texas searching for the woman and baby in wary-eyed towns and long stretches of empty land, always afraid that the past would catch him. He wanted to live now, because somewhere they lived.

Under the faint light of stars he spent half-nights on his knees in prayer, asking forgiveness for his deeds and guidance to the goal of his search. Forgiveness may have been granted. Who could say? His crimes were lost in the confusion that followed the war.

But he never heard a word about them. And finally he quit asking, quit looking, wandered and stopped, wandered and stopped again.

CHAPTER 21

Alta was afraid. She tightened her arms around her sister, sleeping in the saddle, as if to protect them both from whatever bad thing might be in front of them. She missed her brother, might never see him again, but he had insisted on going to find another band of free people. No reservation, no white man's house, for him. She must think of him now as a warrior who sought his own destiny, not the small boy of older times. Her father might yet decide to leave as well. She could see his discontent.

For herself, she would pretend anything, learn new ways if it had to be. But men were different. Honor was the most important thing to them. For men like Falling Rock life without honor was not to be lived. One thing, though, he loved more–his wife and daughters, and that was what held him here now.

And what would become of herself and John and the thing that was between them? The old ways had died–the way you behaved, the way you thought and dreamed, all gone. John was trying hard to become Comanche, but it was too late. He was white in the head. The world around them was moving too fast. But it was true that he was the son of Two Hawks, the great war chief who had fought against the whites since before she was born. John was a man of honor, too, and she was proud that he loved her.

The little girl shifted and stuck her thumb in her mouth. Alta removed it with a tender hand.

It would be her turn now, if the Turner man allowed them to stay, to learn and John's to teach. And the woman, John's mother, she could teach them, too. She had lived in both worlds, so what did it matter how hard it might be? They had all heard the stories of life on the reservations, how the people suffered, starved, how they ran away in great numbers and were caught and taken back like disobedient children, or killed.

This would be better. Honor was good, but for her it was unimportant and now left behind. Her life, the life of tiny *Rabbit* who shared the saddle, her mother, her father with his bowed legs and his head full of dark thoughts. These lives must be saved. They would all learn and live.

Lawrence Billings had easily recognized the two riders–the storekeeper from town and the Turner woman, headed north at a steady gait. He had quit his own search in disgust and was sitting with his back against a rock in the shade of a mesquite tree, whittling a stick and thinking over his situation while his horse grazed in a thick stand of buffalo grass.

They had passed within two hundred yards, so intent on conversation they hadn't noticed him. Minutes later he fell in behind and followed, out of their sight. Watched them approach the hidden cavern and later come out with shouts of anger from the woman.

When they had gone he went inside it himself. Signs of occupation, but no one around now. A stool leaning against a wall. Ashes from a couple of cooking fires. Was this where Boone had been headed? If so he'd come and gone, but where? And what about Harper and the woman? Were they somehow connected to the silver? They had come here for a reason. And they had left angry, disappointed.

This could have been the hiding place of whoever killed the two men and left all those moccasin tracks. It was in the general direction he'd been searching when they had come across Boone. Maybe Boone was part of the killings.

The riders had headed back south the way they'd come. He caught up to them and kept them in sight. When they stopped and made camp, so did he. He could just make out the flicker of their fire through the trees, built none for himself and only slept an hour or two, waiting for them to move on.

In the morning a light rain began to fall, the clean smell of wet cedar bloomed in the air, the branches dousing him with water like shaggy dogs as he guided his horse through them. He carried a slicker behind the saddle, but it was too much trouble, easier to let the rain soak into him. He pressed on. The rain had stopped when he left the trail and made a solitary line to the ranch house.

The trees began to thin as he approached the stone fence of the horse pasture, in almost the same spot Raiford Clawson had watched from days before. Something told him there was a connection here–a connection that could put money in his hand. But he had to be smart and careful, had to think it through.

There was movement on the front porch of the house, but it faced slightly away from him and he couldn't make out who or what caused it. He wished for a smoke, a cup of hot coffee, a plate of beef steak, but those things would have to wait. The sun was scalding hot now and he sheltered himself as best he could under branches, and waited.

The two riders appeared and halted their horses at the porch. Two men came around the corner of the house and stood near them. Too far to make out faces, but one was Turner, with just the one arm. The other had that red-gold hair of the stranger that slapped Leo Manning down. Despite his own discomfort Billings smiled at the memory of that ox in the dust.

The four went inside the house and a few minutes later the storekeeper came back out, got on his horse and started toward town. A moment of indecision; should he follow? No, he knew where to find James later if he wanted him. This was the place to watch Something was going on and if he was patient and careful and most of all lucky, he might find out just what it was. Turner came out and led the woman's horse to the barn, then brought it unsaddled to the pasture and went back in the house.

When the column of riders appeared Billings wasn't sure at first what he was seeing. Cattle? Horses? The rain had begun again, and light had dimmed. The animals in the pasture below him had sought out the corners of the fence and waited there unmoving.

They came from a different direction, over to the northeast, so if they had come from that cave, as he suspected, then they had ridden a wide half-circle, spent twice the time necessary on the trail. And he knew why. They were evading trackers. Evading him. He smiled again. It hadn't worked.

Even at this distance, with the rain and the ebbing light there was no doubt at all. One of those riders was Charlie Boone.

Jezebel rode like a man, her hair piled under the hat, careless in the saddle, used to the motion of a horse. She had not been on one for a year, but had forgotten nothing. It hadn't been hard to find a man in town glad to lend the smooth-gaited traveler. Not hard at all. Men were always too easy, always had been for her.

There was the blazed tree beside the trail. She followed the arrows on the crude map. It would have been better if she had come earlier in the day, because inside the cedar brakes the light was already dimming, and now and then a sprinkle of rain.

She ought to feel more excitement , seeing Raiford again, but the family had scattered so, gone off in their own directions so long ago that the early years seemed more dream than reality. If she could have stolen Dugan's money on her own or known a man she could trust, she'd never have sent the letter in hopes of reaching her brother. But it was done now, better or worse. He was here.

She followed a narrow, winding deer trail that led finally, as most deer trails do, to a water source, a shiny spill from under a slab of limestone, then the pool below, deep enough for the traveler to drink, then the beginnings of a stream, no wider than a man could span with thumb and fingers, that disappeared downhill.

The noise could have come from anywhere, direction confused by the sound of running water, but it was sharp and metallic, the levering of cartridge into rifle chamber.

"Don't shoot. It's Jezzie."

A boot scraped and a man walked out of the trees, a hatless Mexican, dark hair down the back of his neck, a carbine in his hand. "I was waiting for you."

He led her to a ruined structure no more than fifty yards from the spring. One of the walls had fallen, the stones along with chunks of mortar scattered on the ground, replaced by newly-cut branches that both screened it from view and protected the interior. The roof was thatched with cedar branches, needles turned brown. Hobbled horses grazed nearby.

Two men were there. One was her brother.

"Jezzie, you have got even prettier in your maturity." Raif could always come up with words you didn't expect. He took the bridle reins. "Nice looking horse."

"Belongs to a friend in town." Neither made an effort to touch, no hug, no words of kin meeting after long absence.

"Well, this here's Juanito, and the handsome lad we call Goose." Neither man acknowledged the introduction. Raiford tied the reins to a sapling. Rain began to pepper down and they moved inside the safety of the walls.

She handed him a key. "The safe is in his office, across from the saloon you visited, says *jail* over the door, there's a cell or two and bunks in the back, so there's people inside at night and you'll run into a fight if you try it then."

Early morning was best. Everybody was up and out at daylight except Cooter, and he would be no problem. "Don't shoot him," she said. "He's not very bright and you don't have

129

to hurt him." Raiford nodded.

"Might be somebody in a cell, but they'll be locked. And Manning's there. But he's sick from getting shot a while back. Dugan will be having his breakfast across the street in the saloon, so if he looks outside he can see you, but he won't. He spends an hour over his bacon and eggs. All you have to do is go in his office and open the chest or safe or whatever it is, take out the money and leave. Quiet and quick and maybe not a shot fired."

"Where will you be?" Raiford said.

"Waiting for you on this side of the river."

"On your borrowed horse?"

"I reckon he'll be a stolen horse by then."

She returned the traveler to its owner and paid the man with a hug for use of the animal, asked if she might ride again in the morning, learned the location of saddle and bridle, and in her room at last, shed the wet clothing and wrapped herself in a soft, dry gown just as Emil Dugan entered without, as usual, bothering to knock.

Much later, in the small hours after midnight, though, there was a knock. A knock on her door by an unexpected hand.

CHAPTER 22

The sergeant was a pitiful, bedraggled mess, a whipped dog, a prodigal returned. Hungry, too, judging by his eyes, which couldn't keep away from Dugan's food, but the captain offered him none. The morning was wet, gray, humid. Clothing tended to stick, sweat spoiling his fresh-ironed shirt. He considered Billings.

"Of course I refused to talk to you last night. I should have jailed you. You deserted." Billings hadn't tried to sleep when his boss sent him away with threats and harsh words. He had walked the street, waited for daylight, honing and arranging his story. He pulled the silver iguana from a hip pocket, hid it inside the hollow of his hand and showed it to Dugan.

"And just what am I to make of that?" But Billings had seen the flare of recognition in the casual glance.

"I know where the man is that lost it, sir. I've been searching for him all this time. I can take you straight to him."

"Take me? Why?"

"There's others around him, Captain. I can't capture him alone."

"Otherwise you would have, I expect."

"It was always my intention to share with you, sir. But I want half of everything we get out of it. And I want your word on it."

"Well, Sergeant, I don't believe you, but that doesn't matter." He chewed a bit of food and swallowed. "We'll stop our games now. I know what that piece represents. If this man of yours turns out to be the gift bearer you think he is I will halve it with you, my word on it, as you say. Now, where is he?"

Billings hesitated. "With respect, sir, I'll wait til you're ready to go after him."

"Don't trust me? Very well, but keep it just between us. We'll take another man or two along this afternoon. How far away?"

"We ought to leave by noon, give ourselves plenty of daylight."

A gun boomed somewhere on the street. Billings shoved his chair back, almost tipping it over. Men shouted. He drew his pistol and ran toward the door, suddenly free of the sleepiness that had drugged him moments before. A body lay face-down in the doorway across the street. Three men on horseback wheeled their mounts, bent low over their saddlehorns. He stepped clear of the saloon and took aim at the rider whose dark hair streamed behind him in the morning wind. He fired. The rider fell.

Raiford had brought an empty feed sack, and it was a good thing because much of the safe's contents was loose cash and coin, a few gold nuggets, jewelry. The rest was in heavy leather sacks that Goose carried out in two trips and stuffed in his saddlebags. Juan held the horses and watched the street.

Neither Cooter nor the man in back offered any resistance, though Cooter said once, "The captain's gonna be really mad at you." He said it standing in the door as they mounted and prepared to leave. Goose drew his gun and shot him.

The shot cost not only Cooter's life, but Juan's as well.

They crossed the river going all out and Jezzie joined them on the run, worried by the shots she'd heard, not minding the missing man, but wondering if some of the money had stayed behind with him. They rode a mile before stopping, no sign yet of anybody after them. Of course, somebody would come.

Out of breath, Raiford said, "Goose, I've a mind to shoot you myself after what you pulled back there."

The boy smiled. "Try it, then." Blood exploded from his open mouth as a slug pierced his spine and tumbled through the flesh of his throat and cheek, exiting beneath his left eye and killing him instantly.

Raif looked at his sister and the smoking barrel of her pistol. "Well, Jezzie, I deplore this kind of bloodshed, but I reckon it had to be. He was too far over on the wild side. I guess the money's all ours now."

"The money's always been ours, Raif, from the minute that fool told me about it."

They split the take into two parts and she loaded her share onto Goose's pony and left the borrowed traveler tied to a tree. His owner was a nice man who had treated her well, and she had never intended stealing his horse.

"Where you headed, Raiford?"

"California sounds good to me right now."

"I was thinking the same thing. Want to ride together? Be family for a while?"

"Why not? I sort of like the idea." They left Goose where he had fallen. Jezzie thought she saw a tear on her brother's cheek and wondered what sorrow had brought it there.

Dugan, Billings and a half-dozen others chased the thieves all that day and most of the next. Silver stayed on Billings' mind, but the captain could not be deterred. He was near insanity over the loss of his treasure, full of murder for whoever had done it. Finally, late into afternoon on the second day, without food, exhausted, with no hope of catching the pair, they turned back.

One horse died under its rider and the man had to find a seat behind someone else. A wonder more of the animals didn't die, because Dugan kept going homeward without rest. The pace reminded Billings of times during the war when the captain ran men and beasts into the ground, and seemed to love doing it.

They returned after three days and two nights with little rest and so were forced to sleep. Except for Dugan, who learned the whole truth of his loss and lay awake through the night in an empty bed.

On the morning Juanito and Goose died three riders decked out for working the brush were already hard at it, doing the work of honest men. Breakfast was far behind them, and Charlie Boone's quarter horse was earning his keep. Hub watched Ben Turner handle a lariat, bridle reins between his teeth, all of his experience focused on the job they were doing. Hub's mare was fine, though he favored her and didn't ask her for some of the work the others took on. No sense taking unnecessary chances with her leg.

Hub felt good, working at last, doing what he'd come for, and the countryside was full of cattle. Ben knew where to look. Boone was along because he didn't want to sit idle at the house. Not handy with cattle yet, but his horse nearly made up the difference, fast as a mink with a twenty-foot jump.

John had stayed back to help Sarah with the Indians, get them set up in the bunkhouse. There were plenty of beds for all of them. Hub and Charlie had spent the night in the barn, and Hub had liked it there. No reason to sleep anywhere else. The families could have their privacy. He thought maybe the brave, *Falling Rock,* would leave he was so obviously unhappy, and maybe his women with him but for now at least there was less danger to them. He roped a brindle heifer and left her tied with the others until they could collect a herd large enough to drive back to the pen.

James left town the day after the robbery. They'd called him to join the chase and he had declined. Why should he join in recovering stolen money already stolen by Dugan. He was surprised they hadn't returned by this time. Thieves chasing other thieves.

Not good leaving the store unattended again, but he propped

the door open and left a note on the counter in case anybody needed something before he returned in the afternoon. He needed to be sure they were safe at the Turner ranch. He wanted to tell them about the robbery, the shootings, find out if they'd learned anything about John.

Most of all he wanted to talk to Sarah.

She met him at the door and seemed pleasant as ever, glad to see him. *How many of my troubles are in my own imagination?* He wondered.

"They're here."

"John?" The news surprised him. Light had returned to her eyes. The cuts on her cheeks had almost healed, were barely noticeable. The kitchen was hot from the cook stove. Steam escaped from underneath a lid. He smelled stewing meat. She pulled a chair away from the table for him and went over to check the pot. The back of her blouse was soaked with sweat.

He told her about what had happened in town. She said, "He deserved it. I hope they get away."

"Yeah, my feelings, too. Where is everybody?" Not really caring because it was her he'd come to see.

"My dad and Hub Anderson are hunting cattle. They took Charlie Boone along. Johnny's with the girl, I'm sure, he always is, the mother and little Rabbit are down back after pecans. Alta's father–I never know where he is."

"You have a large family."

"Yes, we've become a bunch, haven't we. Well, the Comanches stay to themselves for the most part except for Alta, who is here at the house with John when he isn't with her someplace else." A little of her manner was complaint, a little jealousy, mostly acceptance. "I forgot to offer you coffee, James. Would you like some?"

He left the chair and got a dipper of water. "I think a drink of this is what I want." It was still cool from the well. When he put back the dipper, his decision had been made. Despite the water his mouth was dry, his chest as hollow as a rotten log. It

135

would be now or it would be never.

She was aware of the quick change in him, the resolved fear on his face that told her he was about to ask her again and this time would accept no coy evasion. She had known this time was coming and she'd thought about it for days until the people, the options, the hopes and realities had become so tangled she could no longer bear them, so had stopped the whirling questions and opened herself to fate.

He was so earnest. And good. Did she love his earnestness and goodness? Yes, but what about the other feeling? The feeling she had known so long ago for the man *Two Hawks*? The feeling she had believed lost forever?

"Sarah, I'm asking you again."

He was so afraid of her answer. She had never wanted that kind of power over him. Why couldn't they stay as they always had been, with a feeling between them as close friends loved? Everything was changing.

"It's the last time I'll ask you. And Sarah...this time no answer means *no*."

He had tried to help her with John when the boy had been so impossible. Not many men would have been as patient. Now John himself was becoming a man and his allegiance was to Alta and their future. Letting go of him, her sense of responsibility for him, was hard. Did every mother face these feelings? And Ben, tough as he was, strong and resolute as he had always been, was growing older. How would she manage without him?

"I love you and I want to marry you. That's as plain as I can say it. Will you marry me?"

For a moment she wanted to run out the door, could feel the wind on her face, deep gulps of free air in her lungs. Running. Toward something? Away from something? He took a package from his pocket and in it was a ring with a shining stone.

She went to the window, watched a churn of distant movement. Cattle, their horns and flanks a chaos of color and struggle. Three figures worked with quiet fury to push them

136

forward. One of them stood high in his stirrups swinging a bullwhip, his hat blown behind him, hanging by its cord, bronze hair flying like the stroke of an artist's brush on canvas.

James went home with a weight in his chest and a sense of loss that he thought might never leave him. He'd have to give it time, put a smile on his face, and who could say? Maybe someday another woman would come along who could return his love, the ring might fit another finger. But a long stretch would have to pass first. Every man has his time to ride alone.

CHAPTER 23

Falling Rock surprised the men the following day, rode out with them, sat his horse silently watching for a while and then joined in. He wore only a breechclout and moccasins, handled the wild cattle as if he'd always done it.

Ben said, "Funny looking cowboy."

"Good one, though," Hub said. "I reckon this is much the same as chasing buffalo."

"You think he's friendly as he acts? Or he going to scalp me one night?" The Comanche was tailing a cow out of the brush, forcing her back into the herd. Hub and Ben kept them moving with Charlie Boone on his quarter horse chasing down runaways.

They pushed the bunch to the ranch pasture at noon and stopped for a quick meal. With Ben's knowledge of the country and the help of the other two men the roundup was going better than Hub had at first expected–making up for the time lost. If things kept up like this he was just days away from having enough for a drive to the Brazos. Rested and fed, they went to work again, striking out in an easterly direction this time. With luck they'd make up another herd and be back with them before dark.

I'll miss it here, Hub thought as they rode out in the heat of afternoon. The hill country appealed to him. A horizon that always surprised you, clear water and enough space to move in. But he was the stranger, the one who'd move along, go home and find an old dream to live.

When they headed homeward later a thin cover of clouds had blown in from the southwest and soaked some of the heat out of the sky, but it was still hot. The ground had dried out after the light rains. White caliche dust stirred up by horse and cattle hooves stuck to their sweaty faces and hands. The last cow through the wire gap was a light creamy color with short horns and a mean look in her eye.

Ben swung off his saddle and said, "I've seen every color of the rainbow in these cattle the last couple of days."

Charlie Boone had his hat off, fanning his face. "Down on the Gulf I seen cattle looks like that one. Call 'em brimmers. Got big humps on their backs and they mean, too. Bugs and heat don't bother 'em like they do most cattle. So they put the brimmers with regular cows and out pops a calf that don't get sick from hot weather and bugs."

Hub said, "You always surprise me, Charlie. You've turned out quite the cattleman."

"No, I just been riding around a lot, seen some country, you know."

The Comanche had stripped needles off a cedar branch and was rubbing his pony down with them. Ben said, "I never saw anybody as good with horses as these people."

Sergeant Billings almost felt sorry for the captain. Before the robbery Dugan already behaved in ways that caused some to doubt his sanity, but now...losing that money had done something to him. His face looked hollow, as if there were no bones, no form, beneath the skin. Billings wondered if he'd slept any since their return.

You could never predict him. When they'd gotten the young

139

man buried early in the afternoon and the captain had finished saying words over him, which were mostly lies about devotion to duty and that sort of thing, he had sought out Billings on the walk back and said, "We must investigate the Turner situation immediately."

"I've been saying that, sir."

"We'll go right away. Just the two of us. I don't want anyone..." He looked around. Only a few people were with them. Leo Manning was head and shoulders taller than anyone else, and no longer the man he'd been before the shooting. Almost slender now from days without eating and from the stress of the wound, he walked carefully and quietly. Dugan called him over. "Are you strong enough to ride?"

"I think so, if I take it easy."

"Get a horse, then. Meet us at the river." Manning nodded and moved away at the dismissal. He would have to borrow one.

Dugan said, "If any of the people at Turner's were involved in the fight perhaps he can identify them. Jog his memory, you know."

"Captain, I'd rather not fool with that business just now. The silver..."

"Yes, the silver. It remains the most important item on our agenda, but I'm very curious about the contents of his memory." As always, you couldn't argue with the man once he'd decided something.

It was only intuition, of course, but Dugan had always believed in his ability to discern the unspoken, sniff out the scent hidden from others. Turner's story of finding the battle site, saving Manning, felt too convenient. The old ranchman was lying. Perhaps seeing Ben Turner again was the key that would unlock the information Manning carried. And once the truth was revealed he would know what to do with it.

Rabbit had two dolls, one of them new from Sarah and another of beaded buckskin that her mother had made before she was born. She was playing with them, alone in the parlor when she saw the horsemen through a window. The others were in the kitchen preparing supper. Her mother and sister peeled potatoes while John built a fire in the stove. When the little girl ran in chattering only her mother and Alta understood. Alta said to Sarah, "Men outside."

Sarah hurried the three females into her bedroom and closed the door. "Stay with me, John."

She recognized Dugan and Billings. A third man stood behind them, an unfamiliar face. Dugan removed his hat and glanced at the others, who followed suit.

"Yes?"

"Captain Dugan, madam, to see your father." He gestured toward John. "I see your son is here today. I'd like to talk to him, as well."

This was the thing they'd feared. She could hardly catch her breath. "I'm afraid this is a bad time, Captain. My father's not here and I have John busy with chores."

"May we come inside, please?"

"I don't wish to be rude, but another time would be better."

"The request is official. This is police business and I insist we come inside to discuss it." Dugan forced the door open and the three men walked past them. Sarah felt helpless. Ben and Hub and the others would be coming any time now. She had to warn them.

"Have a seat, then," she said. "Would you like some coffee?"

Dugan said, "We'll stand, but coffee would be welcome if you don't mind. When will your father return?"

She headed for the kitchen and they followed. "John, I need a bucket of water, please. I don't know, Captain, he's working somewhere on the ranch." The three men continued standing in the kitchen, in her way, and she had to dodge around them as she got out the coffee and a pot.

John was longer than necessary coming back and that reassured her a little. He must have gone to warn Ben

Billings walked to the back door and looked out. "He's not at the well."

"You know how boys can be. I'll get it myself."

But then the sergeant said, "Here he comes."

John had two eggs in one hand, the full bucket in the other. "Thought you might need these for supper," he said. He leaned against the wall while she measured the water and coffee and got it on the stove.

Dugan put his hand on the tall man's shoulder. "Look through the other rooms."

"I beg your pardon!" Sarah was suddenly frantic with fear. She wished John would just run out the door. "You have no right to search this house."

"Whose buckskin doll is that on the parlor floor?" His eyes were cunning. Sarah edged toward the back of the room and then she noticed that John had the potato knife at his side, hidden from Dugan and Billings. She couldn't let him fight these men, they'd kill him. A door slammed at the end of the hallway and in a moment the tall man appeared.

"Nobody." Even the one word seemed an effort. It was obvious he wasn't feeling well.

"You don't seem to recognize Mr. Manning," Dugan said. If the news surprised John he didn't show it, but it frightened her even more. She stared at Manning, searching his face, and of course once she knew, it was plainly him though a different looking man altogether. Why had he not sounded an alarm?

"In the event you wonder why he hasn't thanked you for saving his life it's because he has no memory of it." Was that possible? Even so it didn't explain what had just happened.

"Whose, then?" Dugan again. "The doll?"

"Mine," John said. Sarah looked at his hands. No knife. He'd hidden it somewhere. "Mother brought it with us from the Indian camp where I was born. I was about to make a pattern from it."

"On the parlor floor." His disbelief was plain.

"Yes, sir. It's a quiet place to work." The two stared at one another, unblinking.

Alta had been terrified when they ran to hide from the visitors. Living this way you couldn't know what any day would bring, but she had begun to feel safe. She had wanted to change things, had believed their life *would* change, and now the three of them could only wait in this room, trading silent glances.

Then the abrupt footsteps, the open door and the tall man in the room with them, a finger on his lips for their silence, looking past them as if they were not there. When he backed out and closed the door they all held their breath and waited for the shout of discovery, but it never came. Nothing happened. Time passed. Still, nothing happened.

CHAPTER 24

The four were headed for the barn. Ben said, "let's feed these horses a trough of corn tonight, put some bottom on 'em for tomorrow."

Hub rode closer. "Last night I asked Sarah about James, how he is, and she didn't have anything to say. Worried me a little. Is he all right?"

Ben laughed. "He's just fine, I reckon. I mean to say, I have to mostly guess like you do. Sarah don't say a lot to me neither." They rode along in silence for a few paces. "But I do believe they've had a parting of the ways."

"She told you that?" James had been so sure. Hub felt his heartbeat double.

"She kind of halfway did and I kind of halfway guessed the rest."

"Well, you never said a word about it all day."

Ben shifted his hat and wiped away sweat with the back of his hand, reins loose over the saddlehorn. "Was I supposed to?" And then John was in front of them, waving them down with his arms in the air.

They put Charlie and Rock in a small mesquite grove out of

sight of the house and got their promise to stay put until this was finished. At the house Hub followed Ben through the door and there was Sarah's worried face and John standing near her and the men standing around the table with coffee cups in their hands. Dugan's eyes registered the pistol on Hub's hip. He said, "Come in gentlemen. I'm here to conduct an interview with you, Mr. Turner. Official business."

"What about?" Ben said.

Hub thought the tall one looked like the giant Manning without all the extra fat on him. The captain said, "Why don't we go out on the front porch?"

Ben considered it. "All right. Me and Hub need to wash up. Give us a minute." They rinsed away the grit from their hands and faces at the enameled basin and Hub threw the water out the door. Where were those Indian women? Dugan watched him carefully. "It's Anderson, isn't it? You and the boy had better come out with us. You, too, Miss Turner."

Hub realized they were all being herded into one place. Better control that way. The tall man *was* Manning and he looked sick. Dugan pointed Hub and John into chairs on the porch. Sarah stood beside the door, and the captain kept Ben standing without any pretense of courtesy. Billings walked over to stand beside their horses and Manning slowly made his way there, too.

"My sergeant tells me you're sheltering renegade Indians here. And a colored man as well, wanted for robbery."

Ben said, "I don't know what you're talking about."

"I'm ordering you to turn these people over to us now. You can't go against the law, and you know it."

"You can carry your law to the devil. Get off my property and take these other thieves with you." Trouble was coming. Hub was tempted to reach for his gun now, but that might get Sarah or the boy hurt.

"Papa, please be careful."

"Go in the house, Sarah." She ignored Ben's direction. Dugan drew his weapon. From the corner of his vision Hub saw the sergeant do the same.

"Stand up, Mr. Anderson. I said stand." Spit ran down his chin and his eyes had gone wild. Hub thought it best to obey before Dugan opened fire on the whole crowd. To Manning, "Take his pistol." Manning climbed the steps and moved behind Hub and slipped the Colt out of its holster. "Just a precaution, Mr. Anderson. You can have it back when we leave."

To Ben, "You'll come back to town with us and we'll have our discussion there."

"No!" Sarah said, "You can't do this to us."

"The boy, too. When I ask questions I expect answers." Hub had already made up his mind that gun or no gun he would not allow them to leave with Ben and John. He felt a touch in the small of his back, put his hand back there and felt a pistol butt. When he grasped it Manning came out from behind him and took his place again beside Billings. Hub watched him, not knowing what to think. Could he trust the gesture? Dugan pulled handcuffs from his belt, then looked at Ben's one arm and returned them with a disgusted shrug.

"Let's go." He shoved Ben toward the porch steps and motioned to John, but instead of standing John sprang forward, his head aimed at the center of Dugan's chest, the knife a quick gleam in his hand.

The little man moved fast. He stepped back to fire, but Ben was suddenly between him and the boy, grabbing at the gun arm, deflecting aim, and then Hub shot the captain in the left eye, dropping him dead on his feet.

Hub spun to go after the other two before Dugan fell and there was the sergeant with his hands in the air and Manning's pistol at his head.

The gunfire brought the hiding men on the run and the others out of the house. The porch was suddenly filled with people, but Billings only had eyes for Charlie Boone. Charlie walked over to him. "Why you still after me, anyway?"

Billings raised his voice. "This man is carrying stolen silver.

Look in the captains's pockets."

Ben came over. "What're you yelling about?"

"Look in the captain's pockets and you'll see." John found it in an inside coat pocket.

"This thing?"

"Yes, it's stolen."

"But he didn't have it," Ben said. "It was in Dugan's pocket. Maybe Dugan stole it."

"There's more, though. He has more like it."

Ben turned to Charlie. "Any truth to what this man's saying?"

"I stole a horse, a knife and a gun a long time ago, Mr. Turner, and that's all I ever stole. He's tellin' you a lie."

Ben turned back to the sergeant. "I think it's time for you to leave, and carry what's left of your boss with you. And just so you know, I'll report what happened here today to somebody who can do something about it. We've had enough from you people."

Leo Manning spoke up, and his voice no longer sounded weak. "I don't mind carrying the captain back to town. The sergeant here is mostly a good man. He's from up yonder in Ohio and I wonder if maybe he couldn't just ride on in that direction."

Ben said, "What do you think, Sergeant?"

Billings looked at the shining ingot in John's hand. Almost his. "Yes," he said, "I'd like to go home."

Emil Dugan would have been upset that no one mourned his passing. They moved his body to a shaded area a hundred paces from the house and left it there while Leo Manning joined them for supper. The invitation seemed only right to Sarah, who made the supper *and* the invitation, and there were no objections. He ate with good appetite, but explained nothing at the table, and they were content to let it be for the moment.

Not so afterwards, on the porch again with coffee, the blood stain avoided by their eyes, many questions on their tongues. "You were pretending all the time?" Sarah asked. He only nodded. "But why? You were so...mean to us before." He nodded again.

"Hard to explain. It started when I got shot trying to kill the Indians. Innocent people, and I knew it while I was pulling the trigger. It's mighty hard to go in a different direction to what you've gone all your life." He took a deep breath and blew it out.

"Then the boy, here, could have killed me. He didn't. I fell in the creek and nearly drowned. Ben pulled me out. And you nursed me. I was out of my head, but I knew what you did."

"Everything?"

"Everything, yes, ma'am."

How close she'd come that night to murder. He knew she had spared him, but she herself would never be sure why. It could easily have been different. There were only the Turners, Hub and Manning on the porch. The others had drifted away to the bunkhouse, and wherever Charlie went to be alone. He had been quiet all through the meal, something heavy on his mind.

Ben pulled the silver piece from his pocket. "You know about this thing?"

Manning said, "No. I never saw it before."

Ben put it down beside his chair. "Well, then, let's not concern ourselves with it any longer."

It was dark when they broke up and left the porch to help him with the body, hanging it over the saddle of Dugan's horse, the horse shying at the smell of blood, difficult to control. John left them, looking for Alta, and Ben called the hound from beneath the house and went for a walk of his own. Hub started to go with him, but Ben said, "Believe I'd like to be by myself a while if you don't mind, Hub. No offense, I hope."

"No, sir. None." He reclaimed a chair and was alone for the first time all day, but not for long. Sarah came back out with a broom and a pan of water and washed and swept the porch.

"I can't just leave that blood there," she said. Then, "Thank you for what you did today. Don't ever doubt he would have killed my father or son if you hadn't stopped him."

"No, I don't doubt it. I'd do it again." She started inside.

"Sarah?"

In the doorway. "Yes?"

"I heard today that you and James have...that you...well, you're not getting married."

"No, we're not. Why do you mention it?" She walked closer to him. It was becoming darker on the porch and he couldn't see her face.

"Why, all this time I thought you had been spoken for."

"I have never been spoken for. James liked to think so, but I never was, never led him on, never promised him anything." She let the silence grow and Hub didn't know how to fill it.

"If I was to...I mean would you let me court you?"

"And how would you go about that, Hub? Courting me?"

"Sarah, you're making fun of me and I don't know how to do this." He felt words come tumbling out. "You're the most beautiful woman I've even seen. I can't stop thinking about you. I think about you all the..."

"I don't like the Brazos valley, Hub. The land is flat and the water is muddy. I don't want to live there."

What was she saying? "But...my land is on the Brazos..."

"I know that. But is it the most beautiful land you've ever seen? And can you stop thinking about it?" And she was gone. He didn't see her again that night.

The hound and Ben came back from their walk later. Ben wondered if the young man had found the chance and the courage to speak up.

CHAPTER 25

Working the cattle next morning Ben Turner found a moment to ride in close to Charlie. He said, "If that silver thing is yours, I left it on the porch."

"Can't be mine, Mr. Turner. Them people found it somewhere. Me, I ain't lost nothing." The quarter horse leaped after a young bull.

Three figures in blue uniforms waited for them at the house that day when they came in at noon. A lieutenant, who introduced himself as Elwin McEntyre, and two enlisted men he didn't identify, along for his protection. James Harper was there, too, come along to show the way. He spent his time in the kitchen with Sarah, and Hub could hardly pay attention to the soldier for wondering if things were changing again. But last night she had said *no, we're not.* The enlisted men stayed at the corral with their horses while the lieutenant sat with Ben and Hub in the parlor of the house.

"I'm stationed at Fort Sill," he said, "scouting for beef. The army needs meat, and the Indian Bureau needs meat. Indians are starving up there and we can't get enough food. I'm offering thirty dollars a head for beef delivered to the fort before winter."

Ben said, "You guarantee that price?"

"Absolutely, if it's good quality and you get it there before November."

"How many head would you want?"

"I'd say as many as you can drive."

"Five hundred head?"

"Or more."

"At thirty dollars a head, guaranteed."

"That's correct. In writing."

Ben turned to Hub. "What do you think?"

"We don't have five hundred head."

"Son, we can get 'em. Another couple weeks of work."

"Well, Ben, you forget that I plan to take half of 'em to the Brazos." So here was something else to get in the way of his plans. One thing after another interfering...

"And you still can, Hub. I just thought your plans were a little more flexible than that."

"How long would it take to drive a herd up there?"

"Why, it's been fifteen years since I been on a drive, but I think we can hit the Red River in a month and make it on to Fort Sill in two, three weeks, depending on the cattle and the weather." He went on, almost to himself, "Go east and hit the Chisholm trail to the river, follow it east some more, then north."

Hub was calculating in his head while Ben talked. After expenses his share would be...well, several thousand dollars. He wouldn't be broke any more and this country would still be full of unclaimed cattle. "What about a crew?"

"Me and you and John, and I think Rock will go along. Maybe Charlie. Might hire Manning. Need more we'll find more."

Hub understood that Ben would make the drive with or without him. "All right. I'm with you."

The lieutenant drew up the papers and Ben and Hub signed while the officer signed on behalf of the U.S. Army. The three

151

soldiers were invited to eat, but begged off with apologies, having a far distance to travel before night. James returned to town with them. He seemed friendly enough, but Hub could feel the separation between them. It would take a while to heal.

Everything seemed to speed up. They had to have a chuck wagon, and found one at the J Bar ten miles away. A rancher by the name of Johnson loaned it to them on the condition they add fifty of his branded beeves to the drive. Charlie Boone volunteered as cook and began to get the wagon ready for travel. Hub went into town and found Manning sitting quietly outside the saloon. He was sober.

"You retired?" Hub said, staying in the saddle.

"No, too young for that."

"You still want to get back at me for the fight we had?"

"No, it was coming to me."

"You want to go on a cattle drive?"

"Where to?"

"What difference does it make?"

"Well, none, I guess. Yeah, why not."

"We pull out in a week and a half. Get your gear together and come on to the Turner ranch." Hub was wheeling the mare as he spoke.

"You can't scrub it all out. Gets down in the wood, always be a stain. If it bothers you the only thing is to pull up the boards and put some new ones in." Harvey Kitren had seen blood aplenty in his lifetime, watched more than one orphaned child or widow wipe it, soap it, broom it and give up in frustration. The worst stain, of course, was in the mind, and it took years of sunshine before it bleached out. Harvey was a small man, dark with his mama's Cherokee blood, pinched of face, eyes set too close together. He knew that for a fact, from the few times he'd looked into a mirror. He wore his pistol on his left hip with the butt forward for a cross draw if he needed it, but he almost never did.

For him it had never been a matter of courage, though he had always felt courageous enough. Early on he had learned that if you just kept going straight in knowing you would kill the man in front of you if you had to, then the knowledge itself became a force that most adversaries backed down from. He carried a letter from the Governor in his pocket and the star of the Texas Rangers on his shirt.

The ride from Austin had consumed most of two days, alone and not stopping to view the countryside, though it was plenty scenic. This business with the State Police had bottomed out all over the state. Now it looked like they'd fund a ranger force again and set things right. Except for stains you couldn't wash out.

The dead Mexican bandit was Juan Rivera. Harvey was surprised to see him, thought he was making folks miserable up in Missouri. The young one he didn't know. They buried him without a name on the marker.

When Hub rode up Harvey was holding the silver iguana in his hand. "And this is what had Dugan in a lather?"

Ben said, "Far as I know, Ranger. Truth is, he didn't make a lot of sense."

Harvey recognized it, of course. Everybody had heard of *Las Iguanas,* but he was not a man who aspired to wealth, so it exerted no pull on him. "You know what it is?"

Sarah and Hub were silent. "I do," Ben said, but he offered nothing else and Harvey let the subject drop.

"Well, there ain't no doubt the late captain was a confused man. Had his own little kingdom, didn't he."

Ben said, "This man is Hubbard Anderson. He's the one shot Dugan, kept him from killing my grandson."

Harvey shook his hand. "Kitren. Everybody seems to agree you acted in self defense, Mr. Anderson. County's not yet organized though it soon will be, so there's not a judge to consult. All up to me, and I think this is as far as we'll go with the matter. I expect you've seen the last of me." Sarah brought him a dipper of water from the kitchen. He shook hands all around, mounted a saddle horse that looked as stringy and tough as himself and began the trip back to Austin.

Hours later as he paused in the middle of an unnamed creek west of the Pedernales River to let his horse drink, he threw something away– gave it a good toss and heard its heavy splash, though twilight had set in and he did not see where the object landed.

The pace never seemed to slow, but gradually it came together–fifty head of cattle from Johnson, the chuck wagon ready, between five and six hundred head wearing the bent T brand. Sore backs aplenty and growing expectations. John and the Comanche girl walked in the woods holding hands and building dreams out of words. Falling Rock began wearing white man's breeches to supper, and had learned the words *thank you.*

One day it was time to go.

Sarah stood watching under the shade at the corral. Hub rode over. He dismounted and stood next to her. They had hardly talked at all during the preparations for departure. Their conversation on the porch that bloody night seemed unreal to Hub, as though it had never happened. "We're leaving, Sarah."

"I can see that. Watch out for dad and Johnny, will you?"

"Yes. Sarah, when I come back I'll have some money. I know a cotton farmer who'll buy my land. I'll have enough to buy land out here, a ranch. I'll stock it and run it. Please tell me you'll marry me."

It was the first smile he'd seen on her face in a long time. "I will, Hubbard. I'll marry you for sure."

She kissed him, let her body touch his, then stood back. It took a while for him to catch his breath.

CHAPTER 26

The drive took almost all of two months because the Red
River was up from rain and difficult to cross, and the chuck
wagon broke down twice and had to be repaired, and because
of a hundred other things that happened along the way. But
they reached Fort Sill with two weeks to spare, the October
winds already strong and cold.

In a tent outside the fort a boy worked on his hands and
knees, a coat on his back and a knit cap pulled down on his
head. He was separating coats into two piles–one pile for adults
and one pile for children like himself, or even smaller, because
he was not so small.

Eight this year in fact, and he wished Reverend Moore would
hurry back because he didn't like it when the Indian people
came looking for coats and he was all alone in the tent.

He missed his mother. She'd have come, too, if miz Moore
hadn't been so sick, but it was fun in a way without her, sort of
grown up, and besides, he would get to tell her all about it
when they got back to San Antonio. *Too bad,* he would say.
You should have come, too. It would be nearly Christmas then,
the two of them snug in their house near the church with a

cedar tree in the corner and candles for light.

The sound of a passing cattle herd outside brought him to his feet. He liked to watch the cowboys and pretend he was one of them, high up on a horse riding back and forth and yelling and flapping his big hat in the air. One of the cowboys with this herd had a face the same color as his.

They spent half the day counting the herd and signing papers, and when it was finished Ben carried their money out of the fort. There were wages to be paid. Leo Manning was not returning with them. "I've got some ideas I want to chase," he said.

And Charlie Boone was going off on a ride to somewhere on his own again. He wondered had he forgotten the directions old Bill gave him all that time ago. Maybe he had, but he hadn't forgotten where the vest was buried.

Hub and Ben, John and Falling Rock would begin the journey back to the hill country this very day. Every time Hub thought of Sarah and her last words to him, *I'll marry you for sure,* it was all he could do to wait another minute.

Charlie said, "I need to find me a new blanket somewhere. My old one's fallin' apart and this wind is cold."

The private soldier who had accompanied them out of the fort said, "There's a sutler on the other side of the fort. Or, you might try over there." He pointed to the tent. "Church folks up from San Antonio with winter clothes for the Indians. I know they have some blankets. Might sell you one. Heck, might give you one."

Ben paid him out his wages and share of profits. "Be back in a minute," he said, and carried the money in his hand toward the tent.

The boy looked up as the cowboy came inside. Behind him came Reverend Moore, shaking from the cold and laughing at it the way he did, and he called out, "Tom! Let's get a fire going in here. I'm freezing."

The boy wondered why the stranger stood there so still and

why he stared at him so long, looking first at him, then back at the Reverend, face all surprised. Reverend Moore stopped laughing too, like he knew something important was about to happen. And then..."Son." the cowboy said, in a whisper so low you could hardly hear him the way that wind was blowing, "is your mama named Rosabelle?"